PRAISE I

"Thor, Baldacci, Flynn, Hamburg. Get ready as Banner fits right in!"

AMAZON REVIEW

"Move over Jack Reacher there's a new guy taking over."

AMAZON REVIEW

"Great stuff. Exciting and fast paced. On par with Flynn & Thor."

AMAZON REVIEW

"The writing was superior, the story line was compelling and the action was top-notch. Sorry I could only give this one a five star rating!"

AMAZON REVIEW

BLOOD OF THE INNOCENT

A HARRY BAUER THRILLER

BLAKE BANNER

ISBN-13: 978-1-63696-322-8

ISBN-10: 1-63696-322-6

Cover design by: Damonza

Printed in the United States of America

www.righthouse.com

www.instagram.com/righthousebooks

www.facebook.com/righthousebooks

twitter.com/righthousebooks

HARRY BAUER THRILLER SERIES
Dead of Night (Book 1)
Dying Breath (Book 2)
The Einstaat Brief (Book 3)
Quantum Kill (Book 4)
Immortal Hate (Book 5)
The Silent Blade (Book 6)
LA: Wild Justice (Book 7)
Breath of Hell (Book 8)
Invisible Evil (Book 9)
The Shadow of Ukupacha (Book 10)
Sweet Razor Cut (Book 11)
Blood of the Innocent (Book 12)
Blood on Balthazar (Book 13)
Simple Kill (Book 14)
Riding The Devil (Book 15)
The Unavenged (Book 16)
The Devil's Vengeance (Book 17)
Bloody Retribution (Book 18)
Rogue Kill (Book 19)
Blood for Blood (Book 20)

ONE

THE TRUCK APPEARED FIRST AS A SINGLE LIGHT glowing in the blackness of the desert, under the immense expanse of stars in the moonless sky. It moved in a slow zigzag, then slowly morphed and split in two, like a luminous amoeba. Gradually it resolved itself into a pair of headlamps whining and grinding along a desert track. They halted and paused where the anonymous dirt track joined State Route 375, in Lincoln County, Nevada. They paused for a couple of seconds, then lumbered right and headed at a steady fifty miles per hour toward Crystal Springs. The truck was a dull red with no markings, and towed a medium-sized trailer. The bill of lading stated the name of the consignor as Edwards Air Force Base, though that was two hundred and fifty miles to the south and west of where the cargo had been collected, at Homey Airport, otherwise known as Groom Lake, or Area 51.

The consignee was listed as the United States Navy, at the Norfolk Navy Yard, 4701 Intrepid Avenue, Norfolk, Virginia. The quantity of cargo was one, the weight was seven tons, the measurements were twelve feet by nine by nine and the volume was nine hundred and seventy-two cubic feet. The description of the cargo was simply, "Sub-aquatic exploration equipment."

At Crystal Springs the truck picked up US Route 93 headed east, and at Panacea, it turned east again to enter Utah, where it finally connected with the I-15 at Cedar City, almost six hours after it had left the base at Groom Lake.

There were four men in the truck, and all were Delta Force operators. They did not wear uniform, nor did they refer to each other by rank. If you weren't fit to lead, they wouldn't follow you, whatever rank you had. Behind the wheel was Black George, six foot six of solid muscle. In the passenger seat was the man they called NY, not because he was from New York, but because he could group thirty-six rounds into a two-inch bull at ninety yards. He had a black beard like a bramble bush and shoulders like two hams.

Traveling in back with the cargo were Scott, who was small, wiry, freckled and rumored to be indestructible, and Twofer, who practiced Zen meditation and was said to have shot two Taliban with a single round, not once but three times.

None of the operators knew what was contained in the metal box in the trailer, though amongst themselves they had concluded it was either EBEs—Extraterrestrial Biological Entities—parts of a captured UAP destined to be reverse engineered at Norfolk, or, least likely according to their assessment, it was an experimental AACC: an Aerial Aquatic Combat Craft, shaped like a giant tic-tac.

From Cedar City the driving became easier, but they didn't pick up the pace much, averaging fifty to sixty miles an hour, and swapping drivers every six hours. At Sulphurdale they turned onto the I-70, went north as far as Salina and then east. They had been driving for some nine hours; it was one thirty AM. NY was at the wheel and they had left the Colorado state line eight miles behind them. They were three miles short of exit 11, for the town of Mack, coming around a broad bend in the road, when they saw the flashing red lights up ahead.

Their orders were strict: stop for nothing and no one until you reach Norfolk. NY didn't slow. Black George pulled his Sig Sauer P226 from under his arm and spoke into the microphone on his collar.

"We got some kind of barrier in the road up ahead. Red lights, there's a guy in a reflective jacket waving a signal lamp."

The answer came back in his earpiece: "Copy that."

NY said, "There's a truck across the road. I can't get through."

"Shit."

He began to slow. "I either got to ram them or turn around and go back to Utah, pick up the Old US Highway."

"Stop." The two men looked at each other. Black George repeated, "Stop before we get any closer. We need distance if it's a highjack."

NY brought the truck to a halt and reached under his seat for his M4A1 assault rifle. The sixteen-wheeler was fifty or sixty yards up ahead. The cab was facing forward, but the container was angled at forty-five degrees across the road. The guy with the signal lamp had turned his back on them and was facing the distressed truck, where four more men were standing around the cab talking. One of the men appeared to be the sheriff. Black George glanced at the side of the road, by the rear of the sixteen-wheeler. There was a Ford pickup with the Mesa Sheriff's insignia on it.

"Ain't the Mesa Sheriff based at Grand Junction?"

NY nodded. "Yeah, why?"

"We ain't passed Grand Junction yet." He pointed at the Ford. "So how'd he get his pickup this side of the truck?"

The sheriff and the guy with the lamp were walking toward them. Black George said, "Back her up."

There was a sharp, unpleasant noise, like a *spink!* NY let out a soft grunt and sagged. He had a red-black dot in the middle of his forehead, like a Hindu cast mark, and his headrest was spattered with gore. Black George swore violently and spoke into the mic on his collar.

"NY down. We have a hijack."

He grabbed NY's assault rifle, opened the door and dropped to the road. On one knee he double-tapped the guy with the lamp and dropped him. The sheriff was running and the four other guys were training their weapons on him. He double-tapped again and another man went down before a hail of bullets hit the cab. He pulled back and noticed too late the flash of fire from the pickup. Two rounds smacked into him. One into his right eye, the other tore through his chin, ripped open his windpipe and smashed the vertebrae in his neck.

Now the sixteen-wheeler started to straighten up, while four men ran to the back of the hijacked truck. Two heaved open the doors. Staying well behind them, a third covered the door with an automatic rifle from a forty-five-degree angle. The fourth hurled in a gas grenade. The doors were slammed shut again, shutting out the screams of pain from inside as the invisible, odorless VX gas entered the men's bodies, causing violent spasms in their muscles, constricting their chests and causing asphyxia and cardiac arrest in seconds.

Without pause two of the men hauled NY and Black George's bodies into the back of the pickup, then ran to haul open the rear doors of the sixteen-wheeler, lowering a ramp to the blacktop. Meanwhile two more guys clambered into the cab of the high-jacked truck and drove it at speed up the ramp and into the larger container. The Ford pickup followed close behind.

Four minutes after the hit, the sixteen-wheeler was on her way, and the only sign that anything had happened on the road was a small crystal cube of shattered windshield, and by nine AM that morning it was incrusted in the wheel of a Mercedes Benz on its way to Salt Lake City.

The sixteen-wheeler followed the same route NY would have

followed as far as Denver, but there, where NY would have continued along the I-70 to Kansas, Indianapolis and Pittsburgh, and then on the I-76 to Norfolk, the sixteen-wheeler took the Colorado I-76 north and east to merge with the I-80 at Ogallala, on the long, uninterrupted journey to New York.

At the wheel was the man in the sheriff's hat. They called him the Cap because he had once been a captain, though he never specified where or of what. He liked to boast that he had lost count of how many people he had killed, and he liked to linger over the word "people," allowing the full implications of the word to filter through.

It was true. At first he had remembered each one of them, and he had wondered what the average was for a special forces operator. It was hard to tell, but he'd figured it was between one and five. So he had strived to achieve six. And along the way he had discovered that it was easier to clock up kills moonlighting in the private sector, especially in Africa, than in the regular army.

When he'd reached eleven kills he had started to lose track of who they were. The women and the kids tended to linger, stirring a vague, emotional uncertainty in his bowels, but the men just kind of blurred into one. And that was ten years ago.

Nowadays, sometimes he thought about his immortal soul, whether he had one, and what awaited it on the other side. But not often. Mostly he just cycled through work, violence, drink, violence and work again.

The truck hummed and the dark road slipped by.

After a while he looked at the man sitting next to him. They called him Seth. Nobody had a full name. Nobody had a past, except they knew Seth was South African because of his ugly fucking accent. He said he came from Seth Efrika, so they called him Seth. You were what you were in the moment, and that was all. It was kind of Zen in a way. The Cap thought of Zen as the Way of the Warrior. Don't think, don't try, don't even do. Just fucking *be!*

Seth returned the glance and they laughed.

"Fuckin' sweet! Eh, boy?" and after a moment he asked, "Who bought it?

"Carlos..."

"Fuckin' dago. Carlos no-loss. Who else?"

"Wolf."

"Shame. Wolf was good."

"We're all good. When our time comes, we go. That's the story."

They fell silent for a while, thundering through the dark toward New York. After a while Seth asked, "We got four stiffs onboard. What are we going to do with them?"

"We send 'em to Cadiz, in Spain."

"Yuh, I know where Cadiz is."

"The container gets transferred to a smaller ship that belongs to the boss. Somewhere between Ibiza and Sardinia, they stick 'em all in the Ford and dump 'em in the sea."

"What about New York customs?"

The Cap looked at his second in command for a moment. "What's the matter? You getting nervous in your old age?"

"Not especially, Cap." There was an edge of insolence to his voice. "I just like to know where the problems might come from. There is a chance customs will inspect the container at Red Hook before loading it..."

"No, there isn't."

"Why?"

"You ask too many fuckin' questions."

"Yuh, and as long as my life is on the fuckin' line, I'm going to keep askin' too many fuckin' questions."

The Cap sighed. "The Brooklyn docks are run by the mob. You work there, you work for the mob. You have a high-value product you need to get in or out of New York by sea, you gotta talk to the mob. They make it happen."

Seth nodded and grinned. "See? You learn something every day. My mother used to tell me all the time, Seth, don't ask so many fuckin' questions."

The Cap frowned at Seth. "I though you just said..."

"Yeah, but she was an ignorant fuckin' loser!"

They both laughed and the tension was dispelled for a while.

The journey took them thirty-six hours, and at just after one PM Friday afternoon they arrived at Teterboro on the I-80 and merged with the I-95 at the Overpeck County Park interchange. They followed the I-95 across the Bronx as far as Westchester Creek and then turned south through Throgs Neck and into Brooklyn. Finally, at one forty-five in the afternoon they deposited the container at Red Hook Terminal. They paid their dues to the appropriate authorities, paid off the Italian boys and made their way by taxi to the JFK Hilton Garden Inn. There they showered and ate, and Seth retired to sleep for a couple of hours.

Meanwhile the Cap made a call to Marbella in Spain. It was a secure number that only he had. It rang twice and a large voice said, "*Capitan*," grunted softly and went on, "You have good newses for me. You are in New York."

"I have good news for you, Mr. Omeya. The transfer of property went ahead without a hitch, and the goods are now on the dock waiting to be loaded aboard the *Princess Diana*, departing Red Hook, Brooklyn, Saturday at four AM. It will arrive in Cadiz in a week, maybe a little less."

"Good, good. What is happen to the other driver and his friends?"

"We won't be hearing from them again, sir. They are sleeping."

"With the angels?"

"Yes sir."

There was contented laughter on the other end of the line. "Well, well, I am happy. You come back to Spain now. I need you to make some insurance for me before the *Princess Diana* is arrive. I call the *Hesperus* now and she will be here in maybe three or four days to transfer the cargo. I don't want no problem. You must take care of this for me, eh, *Capitan?*"

"Don't you worry about a thing, Mr. Omeya. I will take care of everything. You know you can depend on me."

"OK, *mi Capitan*, is very good. I will see you tomorrow, then."

He hung up and the captain allowed himself a couple of hours' sleep before he called Seth and they headed for the airport, and European departures.

The *Hesperus* was a Greek registered, medium-small container ship that Baldomero Omeya owned. Baldomero Omeya was based in Marbella, though his ship operated mainly out of Piraeus, in Greece. The ship, like the man who owned it, was borderline legal and dealt in a couple of billion dollars in a bad year. The captain of the *Hesperus* knew that at least half of his trade was in arms, and a big chunk of the other half was pure opium and came from Afghanistan, via the Kalat nature reserve in Pakistan.

In some places, like Pakistan, Russia, Mexico and Italy, you could rely on local mafias to ensure the safe passage of your goods. Other places it was not so easy, and that was where the Cap came in. It was his job, amongst other things, to ensure the safe passage of Don Baldomero Omeya's products through ports where they might otherwise run into trouble.

And that was what he was going to have to attend to now. If the *Princess Diana* had docked in Malaga, a small bribe would have taken care of things. But Cadiz was a different proposition. The *Guardia Civil*, and in particular the new head of the Andalusian *Guardia Civil*, General José Ferrer García, had the ports of Cadiz and Algeciras gripped in a steel glove. They had seen how the Russian Mafia, trafficking drugs from Morocco, had turned Marbella and Malaga into cesspits of corruption, and they were determined that the same thing was not going to happen in Cadiz. So it was his task, now, to convince the general that certain ships and certain transactions were best simply ignored.

As they soared high above the black waters of the Atlantic, the captain looked down at the ocean falling away beneath them and he smiled to himself. The supreme commander of the Andalusian

Guardia Civil, the great and good General José Ferrer García, would be sobbing and begging, by the time he had finished with him, just to be allowed to assist Don Baldomero Omeya in any way that he could. He would see to that. This was just another job, like any other.

TWO

She was the most beautiful creature I had ever seen. Her hair was a rich, opulent brown with flecks of black, her eyes were a deep, golden caramel. Her head was slightly turned to watch me. We remained like that for a timeless moment. There was utter stillness. The only sound was the crystal cold lapping of the brook where she had stopped to drink. I knew that within seconds she would probably lunge at me and tear me to pieces, but at that moment it seemed to me to be a perfect time to die.

She was big, probably four hundred pounds, three and a half foot at the shoulder and an easy six foot six if she stood upright. She was no more than thirty feet away. I averted my gaze to show I did not want a confrontation. She was too close for me to run, and though she'd be an easy shot, and I had the arrow nocked, there was no way I was going to kill her.

She hesitated. By the first week of December most bears in Wyoming are already hibernating. And this year the snow had been exceptionally heavy, but something had disturbed this grizzly, which meant she was going to be either really mad, or really sleepy. So I stayed in plain view, looked away and licked my lips. I was trying to tell her, with my body language, I didn't want any trouble. I wasn't challenging her, I didn't want to eat her and I wasn't planning an ambush. All I wanted was a drink, when she was done.

For a moment it looked like maybe she'd buy it. She turned back to the water. Then her ears went back, her snout curled and she turned and stood. The noise she let out was terrifying, somewhere between the braying of an elephant and the roar of a lion. I figured she wanted me to go away, so I backed up a couple of steps and hooked my fingers on the bowstring. I knew if I ran I was dead. But I also knew I was going to hesitate too long about killing her. So I was probably dead anyway. I backed up another step and looked away. I could feel the branches of the trees prodding at my back. My heart was pounding hard, high up in my chest.

She didn't move. She remained standing, staring at me, her snout creased to show huge, yellow, savage teeth. I kept looking away and took another step back. Branches cracked and snapped. Then she roared again, dropped to all fours, lunged forward so she was just fifteen feet from me and I could smell her hot breath. I knew I was dead. It was too late to shoot. She reared up again and my head was full of the terrible noise of her bellowing. I pulled and tried to aim, but my whole vision was filled with her massive form.

Then she had turned away, on all fours again, and she ran, lumbering, splashing across the stream and bounding in among the trees. And the air was filled with another, louder, deafening noise. The trees were bowing and bending, the air was gusting in powerful eddies and the thud and throb of a chopper invaded the peace of the mountains. I released the bowstring and hunkered down to take several deep breaths and steady the pounding of my heart. There are many ways to die. Being torn apart by a grizzly is not in my top five preferred choices.

I stood and stepped out into the clearing, looking up into the low-slung gunmetal clouds. I could see the chopper hovering less than a hundred yards away. It wasn't Search and Rescue. It was private, and I couldn't think of a lot of reasons for a private chopper to be hovering low over the Wind River Mountains in early December, unless it was somebody from Cobra looking for me.

There was a guy in dark shades sitting beside the pilot. He pointed at me and the chopper came in close, looking for a place to put down in the snow on the clearing. I knew the area from previous years and I pointed to a spot I knew was more or less flat. He came in, making a blizzard as he did so, and settled down on the ground. The snowstorm drifted away as the rotors thudded to a halt, and the passenger door opened. The guy who climbed out was probably six-one, broad-shouldered and obviously military. I knew him. He raised a hand and I started walking toward him. I said:

"Captain Russ White, US Air Force. What the hell are you doing out here?"

"Harry, good to see you. I might ask you the same question. Any objection to lunch in Pinedale? I took the liberty of having your camp rolled up and slung in the chopper. I'm afraid I have to take you back to New York."

"I just got here."

He laughed and slapped me on the shoulder. "You got here a week ago. Isn't that enough of living in a bivouac and shitting in the snow?"

I sighed and unstrung my bow. "Not really."

We climbed into the helicopter and the pilot took us up and we rose above the trees in another blizzard of snowflakes. I looked for the bear as we circled and headed west of south, toward Pinedale. I didn't see her, but I hoped she'd made it to her den, and would be able to sleep.

Russ leaned in and shouted above the whine of the turbine and the thud of the rotors. "*Was that a bear we saw? Did you see it? He was pretty close!*"

I smiled and nodded. *"I saw her. We had a chat, but you scared her off."*

He laughed. *"Should I apologize?"*

I smiled, but I didn't answer. I wasn't sure myself.

We put down at the Burger Barn, a remote burger restaurant about half a mile outside Pinedale. Russ jumped out and told the pilot we'd meet him at the Wenz airfield in a couple of hours. I climbed out after him and, huddled into our coats, we made our way to the barn.

Inside, in the warmth, Russ ordered a hamburger and I got a bison steak. We got a couple of beers and grabbed a table by the fire. I pulled off half my drink and sighed. Beer is one of the things you miss. After a moment, I said:

"I was supposed to have a month's break."

He shrugged and gazed at the flames for a moment. "What can I say? It's not my department, but you seem to be in demand."

"What's it about? Do you know?"

"You'll have to see the brigadier and the colonel, but I can give you the bones."

"Go ahead. I'm listening."

"You've heard of Groom Lake?"

"Have you heard of the Sleeping Beauty? Of course. Area Fifty-One, it's part of our folklore, like Buffalo Bill, Custer and Geronimo."

"Right, so, even though the government does not officially acknowledge its existence, it exists, and they conduct highly classified, cutting-edge military experiments there."

I drained my glass and waved it at the bartender. Russ sipped his drink and went on.

"So Groom Lake has been working on a project for the last fifteen years or so in collaboration with the Navy. Don't ask me what it is, because I have no idea, but word is it is near completion. My guess—and that's all it is—is that it's some kind of device which operates in the air as well as in the sea."

"Makes sense."

I leaned back so the waiter could place our plates on the table. He took my glass and replaced it with a full one, spilling foam over the edge. He told us to enjoy and went away.

"Yeah, s'what I think. So, Wednesday, this thing, whatever it is, ships out from Groom Lake in an unmarked truck, after dark, with only a small handful of people in the know."

"Ships out where?"

"To Norfolk, Virginia, the naval shipyard. Not even the commanding officer at Norfolk knew the exact date and time of shipping, or the route it would take. But somewhere along the way, probably before reaching Denver, the truck was hijacked. Now, nobody knows where it is."

"How'd we find out?"

"The Delta team were supposed to check in with Groom Lake Friday afternoon to say they had delivered the goods. Commanding officer at Norfolk was supposed to confirm with a simultaneous call. But when she called it was to say the goods were late. The Delta team have disappeared and so has the truck. No trace."

I chewed for a moment, then took a pull on the beer.

"So are we thinking the Delta team took it?"

He shrugged, picked up the burger and examined it, like he was looking for a weak spot he could assault. "I don't know what the brigadier's thinking, but that's sure as hell what I'm thinking." He took a large bite and chewed, wiping ketchup from his mouth. "The alternative is that Groom Lake has a leak. And I don't buy that."

I laughed. "I wonder if Bob Lazar would agree with you."

"Who?"

"Never mind. A mythological character. So, if we don't know where the goods are, or where the Delta team is, what do they want me for?"

He grinned, forced himself to swallow and took a long pull on his beer.

"The brigadier says he is pretty sure he knows who orchestrated it. And that's about all I know."

There was a Learjet 45XR waiting for us at the Ralf Wenz Airfield, about four miles outside Pinedale. My stuff had already been loaded aboard and we made Teterboro Airfield in New Jersey in three hours and forty-five minutes. There was a Jaguar waiting for me with a chauffeur, who saluted and took my kitbag. Russ shook my hand and told me he was parked outside and he'd see me around.

The chauffeur slung my bag in the trunk and opened the rear passenger door for me. I climbed in and saw there was a glass panel between me and the driver. He got behind the wheel and the latches went down. The brigadier had fed me what he wanted me to know in advance via Captain Russ White, of the US Air Force. Now he didn't want me talking to anybody else, or anybody else talking to me.

We drove at speed across the George Washington Bridge and then at a brisk pace down Amsterdam as far as West 110th, and then continued at an equally brisk pace down Columbus as far as West 76th, where we turned in and stopped outside a Cobra safe house I had visited before. It was the kind of safe house you'd expect from the brigadier. Other safe houses are grim, cheaply furnished slums. But the brigadier had this idea that those were exactly the kind of places you would expect a safe house to be. What nobody would ever expect was a brownstone on West 76th, two hundred yards from the park with a Jaguar parked out front.

I guess he had a point.

While the driver delivered my kit to the basement, I climbed the ten steps to the heavy, oak door and rang the brass bell. After a short wait it was opened, and by a man I had seen before. He wore a white jacket and white gloves, gave a small bow and raised his eyebrows at my attire, which was more suited to hunting with a bow in the Wind River Mountains, than visiting brigadiers on the Upper West Side. I followed him across an amber marble floor, strewn with Persian rugs, to the study. It was as I remembered it, all oxblood leather and dark wood, overlaid with the sweet smell of aromatic pipe tobacco.

The brigadier was sitting by the fire, with the flames reflecting in the cut crystal tumbler he had on the occasional table beside him. He looked startled when I came in, and stood, striding toward me with his hand outstretched.

"Harry, so sorry to call you back from your vacation. Have you eaten?" He glanced at his watch. "Glass of whisky and some sandwiches?" He didn't wait for me to finish but looked past me at his man in the white coat. "Plate of sandwiches, trout, ham, cheese, pickles… You know the sort of thing."

"Suited to a whisky, yes sir."

The brigadier gestured me to a chair. "Jane is abroad, otherwise she'd be here. This is a very delicate business, Harry." I sat while he poured me a drink. It was good to be beside the fire and I welcomed the whisky.

He returned to his own seat and repeated, "Very delicate indeed."

"A Delta Force team have stolen a flying saucer from Area 51. That's pretty delicate. But what's it got to do with me?"

He narrowed his eyes at me for a while, like he was trying to remember why I was there. Finally he drew breath.

"As you say, we tend not to get involved in those issues. However, this theft, this hijacking…"

"Forgive me, sir, but a theft is one thing and a hijacking is another."

His eyebrows rose high on his forehead. "Apparently you think I am not aware of this."

"I'm sure you are. But in this case, a hijacking would involve somebody snatching the truck from the Delta Team. I have trained and worked with guys from Delta on many occasions, as have you, and we both know it would not be easy to snatch a truck from those boys. A theft, on the other hand, does not require a third party. They could do that all on their lonesome."

He nodded and sipped. "That is of course true. However, I

am assured by both Groom Lake and a close friend at the SFOD that this team are beyond suspicion. And furthermore I have reason to suspect a very particular person. And I need you to find that person, interrogate him and then kill him. But it is imperative that it look like an accident."

I frowned and sipped. "Imperative?"

"Yes, you see, his brother is Pablo Martinez." I made an "I don't know" face, shrugged and shook my head. He said, "The president of Spain."

I frowned. "They have a president? I thought they had a king instead."

"They call him the president of the government, but he is in fact more akin to a prime minister. But the point is, we of the Anglophone Five Eyes should not go around killing the brothers of presidents or prime ministers of other Western democracies."

"Not cricket?"

"Definitely not cricket. Particularly as the European Union is rather unhappy with the Five Eyes nations since Brexit, and especially since Australia dumped France's submarines in favor of ours." He took a moment to chortle, then went on. "So, you will understand that it is extremely important that this man's death appear to be an accident."

I nodded. "I understand." I cleared my throat and drained my glass. "Do I understand also that you suspect the European Union has stolen...whatever this is, from the US Air Force?"

He sighed. "I honestly don't know, Harry."

THREE

"So who is this guy?"

He stood and made his way to his desk, where he picked up a blue folder and brought it over to me. I opened it and the first thing I saw was a large photograph, roughly eight by eleven, of a big man in his late fifties. He had crew-cut gray hair, big jowls and a large nose. His eyes were so dark they looked almost black, and his skin was a deep olive. He looked more Arab than Spanish. He was wearing a tweed jacket and an open-neck shirt, and his expression as he looked at the camera was one of veiled contempt. The brigadier sat.

"Baldomero Omeya, born in Cordoba in 1967, middle-class family. Pablo Martinez, the president, is his half-brother. Same mother, Angeles Sanchez, but different fathers. Martinez's father was a northern industrialist from Bilbao, one Juaquin Martinez. Omeya's father was a merchant from Casablanca who had a brief affair with Angeles and disappeared when he discovered she was pregnant. They were both educated at Opus Dei schools—"

"Seriously?"

"Yes, they are quite the thing among the Spanish upper class. Martinez was sent to the University of Santiago de Compostela, and his father went to great lengths to promote his career in politics. He is now the leader of the Spanish PSOE, the *Partido Social-ista Obrero Español*. That is the Spanish Workers' Socialist Party. He is also, as I have said, the president of the government."

"Meanwhile, his brother became a billionaire."

"Precisely. He left school at sixteen, though he had stopped attending school long before that. It is not clear when he started trafficking in drugs, but from what we can gather from the *Guardia Civil* and the CIA's investigators on the ground, he probably started selling marijuana when he was thirteen. He, needless to say, was not sent to university. He was briefly involved in a couple of gangs—"

"This was in Malaga?" I was scanning the pages and the photographs as he spoke, absorbing the information.

"Yes, in Marbella. He soon discovered that he could cross over to Morocco and buy hashish cheap and, using his stepfather's name, he was able to get through customs without being stopped. Again, using his stepfather's reputation, he was able to start selling to the top end of Marbella society."

"Come over for a barbeque Saturday and do bring your charming son."

"That sort of thing."

"And before long his friends' parents were asking him if he could get coke as well as marijuana."

The brigadier nodded. "It isn't clear whether he had made contact with his father in Casablanca or not, but he seems to have had some kind of help in Morocco, not just in procuring marijuana but also in acquiring opium and cocaine. What is clear is that by the time he was eighteen he had developed a number of international contacts, and he was making a great deal of money. Enough, in fact, to buy a small apartment in Gibraltar and open a bank account there, safe from the scrutiny of Spanish and European authorities. This was when his criminal career started in earnest."

I spoke without looking up, still studying the file: "He bought a boat?"

The brigadier laughed. "Oh, he did a lot more than that. I think by the time he was eighteen he was looking well into the future. Yes, he had bought a boat capable of crossing the Atlantic, and, by paying suitable bribes both in Morocco and in selected ports in the Caribbean, he was able to start importing large amounts of cocaine into Morocco. Getting it from there into Spain was of course easy. Now he started making serious money, but that serious money also started attracting problems."

I dropped the file on the table beside me and picked up my drink.

"I'd imagine that his stepfather's name was beginning to wear a bit thin with the authorities. One thing is a couple of pounds of marijuana. Another is several Ks of cocaine."

"Precisely. That, and there was also the fact that Marbella already had some very well established providers of cocaine, who happened to be Russian, and were not very amused by this upstart who was trying to horn in on their market."

"Yeah." I nodded. "As I understand it Marbella is a pretty crowded marketplace. There are two or three mafias at work there."

"The Russians, the Romanians and the so-called Manchester Mafia, who despite their somewhat comical name, are a very ruthless, dangerous bunch."

"So what happened?"

The brigadier nodded for a bit, his eyes abstracted.

"It was masterful, really. Through his connections in Morocco, he made contact with a number of Islamic groups in North Africa and the Middle East. He offered them cheap weapons, which he could buy on the black market in Central and South America, in exchange for help and support in Andalusia, and agreed on a deal with them.

"Meanwhile, he made a peace offering to Peter Russov, the head of the Russian Mafia in Marbella. Ten kilos of premium-quality cocaine and two of his main operators, plus the promise that he would withdraw from the market. In exchange he asked for peace, and the guarantee that there would be no reprisals. The deal was agreed. The cocaine was handed over, the unwitting delivery boys were tortured and killed as an example, and peace was declared.

"Two days later Russov's Bentley exploded with his wife and two children in it. His mansion was broken into and his entire staff was murdered. He was tortured and his dismembered body was hung from the gate of his villa. The message was clear. And from that time on Baldomero Omeya has occupied the top spot in Marbella. If you want to do business there, you have to talk to him."

"So how does he get from there to billionaire arms dealer?"

He spread his hands. "He had all the pieces. All he had to do was put them together. It was not hard, with the backing of his new friends in Saudi, Syria and other parts of the Middle East, to prevail upon both his stepfather and his half-brother, to keep law enforcement off his back and allow his boats, such as they were back then, to enter and leave Spanish waters without interference. The risk to his brother was twofold. First and foremost there was the physical risk to him and his family, but secondly—though no less serious—was the risk to his career if Baldomero was exposed. So they came to an understanding: Pablo Martinez would protect his brother, so long as his brother, Baldomero, maintained a public persona of respectability. And that has been going on for over thirty years. And the more Pablo advanced in politics, the more powerful did Baldomero become as an arms dealer and a drug trafficker. Of course his legitimate business as a security firm and weapons broker, which he established shortly after he eliminated Peter Russov, was the front for a much deeper business which spanned—indeed spans—the Middle East, North Africa and all of Latin America."

"OK, that much is clear, but I have a question. What sets this guy apart from so many others? Russov was probably just as bad as this Omeya guy. Why is Cobra interested in him?"

The brigadier drained his glass, smacked his lips and sighed. "I am glad you asked, Harry. Atrocities, crimes against humanity, occur more often that even you might think." I arched an eyebrow and he laughed. "I know, you have lived on the front line and you have seen things no one should ever have to see. But these things happen on an almost daily basis. There are huge sections of the planet where oppression and torture are commonplace, a part of daily life. In parts of Africa boys as young as eight are taught to kill by forcing them to shoot prisoners. In parts of the Middle East, children as young as twelve are taught to decapitate living victims. And the same people who commit these atrocities, routinely annihilate entire villages..." He paused and looked at the fire a moment, then shook his head as though he disagreed with the flames. "I want to say that they do it for no reason." He turned to look at me. "But I don't believe that is the case. Neither do I believe it is a religious thing. I think they do it because they have developed a lust for killing. They achieve a level of excitement when killing weak, vulnerable people, which they cannot achieve in any other way. It is a flaw in the human character, it has been going on since the dawn of human civilization, but in the last thirty or forty years it has reached proportions that are..." He paused again, lost for words. "*Obscene,*" he said at last.

I nodded. "I believe you. But how does this tie in with Omeya?"

"I'm getting there."

He stood and went to pour himself another scotch. He turned and showed me the decanter. I shook my head.

"In order to sell weapons, you need to have conflicts. And as I am sure you are aware, there are huge portions of the globe where there are no more conflicts." He put the stopper back in the decanter and turned to face me again. "In fact the conflict zones are pretty much limited to the southern borders of Russia, the Middle East and certain parts of the African continent." He gave a dry, humorless laugh. "Peace is spreading like a virus, bringing its own problems with it, so what is a poor arms dealer to do?"

"He creates conflicts."

"And he feeds the existing ones, making sure that neither side is ever so well equipped that it can claim victory."

I frowned. "Feeds them how?"

"Over the years he developed a unique technique. As well as arms, he supplied mercenaries. Certain teams of these mercenaries accepted their paychecks from their employers, but actually never stopped working for Omeya. They were merely subcontracted out to Russia, Serbia, Chechnya, Georgia...whoever was hiring them, but with the strict instructions to commit atrocities that would be attributed to their *alleged* employer—"

"Russia, Serbia, Chechnya, Georgia..."

"Precisely, the purpose being to stir hatred, resentment and or defiance in their enemies, to whom he would then sell more arms and mercenaries."

"Jesus..."

"Indeed. This reached its height in Africa, where the so-called international community—meaning the United States, Britain and Europe—are slow to act. One thing is a village massacred on European soil, quite another is a village massacred in Mozambique, Cameroon or Nigeria. Recent intelligence which we have received shows that he has been doing this for some thirty years, on an ever expanding scale. That, for me, would be enough. But what put the seal on it, Harry, was that about ten years ago, he started targeting children. This, he reasoned, would provoke the most violent reaction from the victims, and make them most willing to purchase his weapons in order to exact revenge from the enemy. We estimate that he is directly responsible for the massacre of at least two thousand children in Africa."

"Directly responsible..."

"Mercenaries acting directly on his instructions."

"Consider it done."

He raised a hand, telling me to wait. "There is another facet to this. The weapon that was stolen from Groom Lake."

"How do you know it was him?"

"We don't, and that is just the point. I suspect it was him, but I don't know."

"Why do you suspect it was him?"

He shrugged, spread his hands. "Process of elimination. I don't believe it could be anybody else. Neither the Russians nor the Chinese could have mounted an operation like that inside the United States without our getting wind of it. Whoever did it must have had two things: they must have had equipment already in the country that they could use—"

"What kind of equipment?"

"Well, the team had instructions to stop for nothing and no one. Yet the container lorry vanished without a trace. That means the road must have been blocked completely, and they were either loaded into another, larger container, or they were airlifted out by a Chinook or similar—which I find frankly unlikely, but not impossible. Now, mobilizing that kind of hardware within the States, without being noticed, would be very difficult indeed for a foreign power."

"So it would have to be done by somebody who already had access to that kind of hardware within the United States."

"Precisely. And in addition to that, whoever it was would have to have inside information. Groom Lake has the highest level of security anywhere in the world, Harry. Yet somehow the hijacker knew when the weapon was shipping, and what route it would follow."

I made a skeptical face. "Omeya fits that bill?"

He nodded. "There are security firms in America that have the capability in terms of hardware, but their standing and their reputation are essential to their success, and they are very, *very* closely monitored by the intelligence community. Then there are second-rate, shady operations that sell guns and low-level weapons in Latin America. But they simply haven't the capability or the clearance. Omeya not only owns OTWS—"

"OTWS?"

"Omeya Trans World Shipping, based in Texas, but because of

the global nature of his arms deals and his political connections in Europe, he also has the kind of contacts within the military-industrial complex where that kind of leak might be sprung. I just can't think of anybody else who ticks all the boxes the way he does. Plus...," he shook his head, "he is insane enough to do it."

"Isn't this a job for the Company, sir?"

He gave a soft grunt. "Yes, but I am afraid I just don't trust them. Some of them are very splendid people, and some of them aren't. They'd probably end up stealing it themselves and selling it to a Mexican drug baron in exchange for seven tons of cocaine. Before we knew it the damn thing would show up in Iran." I smiled and he went on. "Now, before you execute him, I need you to find out if he took it, where it is and what he plans to do with it. Once we have that we can inform the president and have Delta move in and exact their revenge."

I nodded. "Yeah, sure. I'll do that. How dangerous is this thing?"

He was quiet so long, staring at the fire, I began to wonder if he was going to answer me. Finally he said, "Very dangerous. I have not been acquainted with all the details. I think only a handful of people know precisely what it is. It was developed at the airbase, so clearly it is an aircraft, and it was on its way to Norfolk where it was to be tested as an aquatic craft. And as far as its weapons systems are concerned, all I know is that until now they have existed only in the sphere of speculative science fiction."

I sighed and drained my glass. "The old cliché," I said, "it must not fall into the wrong hands."

"It must not, under any circumstances, fall into the wrong hands, Harry." For a moment his eyes drifted back to the red flames. "Assuming it is not already in the wrong hands."

FOUR

So, three days after the *Princess Diana* pulled out of the Red Hook Channel and into the Upper Bay, with Lady Liberty standing defiant in the predawn, two miles away on the starboard side, I walked out of arrivals at Malaga Airport, three and a half thousand miles away in southern Spain.

The province of Malaga is more than a little bit like Southern California. Even in December the sun was shining above the palm trees in a perfectly blue sky, and just about everyone you saw in the vast, echoing marble and glass airport looked like they were either on their way to the beach, or returning from it. Straw hats, straw baskets, sunglasses, bare legs and Havaianas were everywhere.

I collected my Range Rover from Rentlux and made my way out of the airport and onto the *Avenida de Velazquez*, which would take me west along the coast toward Marbella.

It was a thirty-mile drive through arid sierra on the right, and the vast sweep of the turquoise Mediterranean on the left, shattered by the silver glare of the sun. And where the sierra swept down to the ocean, it was dotted by walled villas shaded by palms, towering eucalyptus and pines. Further down, the beach was a continuous urban sprawl with no neighborhoods, no central squares, no heart; just mile after mile of casinos, clubs, bars, restaurants and residential areas, geared to take as much and give as little as they possibly could while they lasted. It was, maybe, less like California and more like LA, only without the oil and without the movies.

Marbella itself always reminds me of a beautiful woman who has been raped so often she no longer knows who she is, or why she even exists. At the heart of the city was the ancient Alkazaba, built by the Umayyad Caliph Abd-al-Rahman I, the atheist, maverick one-eyed poet, conqueror of ancient Cordoba. Like an Arabic Odin, red-haired and blue-eyed, he crossed the Sahara on foot after his entire clan was massacred in Palestine. Then crossed the Straits of Gibraltar and built an empire that fostered science, learning, mathematics and poetry. He refused during his reign to build a mosque in Cordoba, but finally authorized it at the end of his life, under pressure from his grand vizier. He insisted, however, in defiance of the law, that it point southeast instead of east. He was my kind of Caliph.

His mosque stands today with a Catholic cathedral at its center, but the Alkazaba of Marbella lies in ruins, fallen from its former glory, surrounded by a minor, shabbier, sadder version of Tinsel Town, complete with its plastic surgeons, plastic people and thriving rehabs.

I made my way to the so-called Golden Mile, and there to the Puente Romano hotel. It was more like a small village than a traditional hotel, with winding cobbled paths and cute, fairy-tale bridges over a babbling brook. The rooms were mostly like small, whitewashed villas, jumbled randomly among exotic gardens. I checked in, dumped my stuff in my room and found the bar, where I sat over a pre-luncheon martini studying the file the brigadier had given me.

Omeya lived in a mansion in the foothills of the *Sierra de las Nieves*, in an outer suburb called *La Montua*. His was the highest, the pinnacle, in a series of sprawling mansions that swarmed up a large bluff between two arroyos that ran down from the mountains north of Marbella. Behind him was a pine forest that spread for some two hundred square miles as part of the *Sierra de las Nieves* national park.

The house itself was set in about five acres of pinewoods and included a large swimming pool set among exotic gardens, a tennis court and a bit of wild woodland to feel wild in. The whole place was enclosed by a fifteen-foot wall topped with razor wire, with cameras set every hundred feet monitoring the wall and the wire. The main gate was solid steel and topped by spikes that looked sharp.

From the photographs taken from high-flying drones, I could make out that he had armed guards in the grounds. I counted six. The house had a large terrace above the entrance, overlooking the gardens and the pool, and there I could see two guards with assault rifles. A smaller terrace at the back, overlooking an Italian garden and the tennis court beyond, also had two armed guards. Ten altogether, plus probably two more inside to make it an even dozen.

I set down the folder and sipped my drink, gazing out at the winding, cobbled paths and the small stone bridge among rosebushes, yucca, palms and pines. To take him out in the house would involve a protracted firefight, and a trail of bodies that would suggest anything but an accident, and would cause his brother, the president, extreme professional embarrassment. That, clearly, was not the job.

I would have to find a different approach, and leafing through the file I thought I knew what that approach might be. Her name was Rafaela Omeya, she was twenty-something, with a faultless, classical beauty that was almost breathtaking and the kind of body that draws the gods down out of the mountains to play house with humans.

In the photograph I was looking at, her hair was thick and black, drawn back into a bun, low down at the base of her neck.

She had eyes that were so dark they looked black too, and very red lips curled into a smile that was as arrogant as it was alluring.

According to the notes Rafaela's hobbies were riding, tennis, skiing on snow and water, and shopping at Puerto Banus. I smiled to myself. I knew how to ski, on snow and water, I was a fair horseman and I could knock a ball around a tennis court. That meant Rafaela and I had a lot in common. We might even just bump into each other on Puerto Banus, shopping for Armani sunglasses.

The file didn't state exactly what her relationship with Omeya was, but it was a fair assumption she was his daughter.

I went to my room and retrieved from the false bottom of my bag some of the equipment I had packed back in New York before departing. When your target is a billionaire recluse in a fortified mansion, chances are high you're going to want to know when he comes in or out. So I had packed a nano-video camera that was triggered by a motion sensor. It was connected by a live feed to my laptop, which would record whatever the camera filmed, and relay images to my cell. I'd also pocketed some other electronic toys I thought might help to get a little closer to my target.

I slipped the camera and a few other gadgets in my jacket pocket and took a drive up *Calle Santillana del Mar*. There I joined the AP-7 freeway, going east and after two miles I came off at exit 184 and turned north up *Calle Padre Paco Ostos*. I wound my way steadily uphill among villas that ranged from pokey "I'll pay anything to have the right address" boxes to veritable monuments to bad taste, complete with Roman columns, Greek statues and Arabesque gardens. Eventually I came to a fork in the road. To the right was the *Camino de los Trapiches*, and to the left was the narrower, less frequented, Calle Montua.

I took the road less taken and began a steady, winding climb through dense pine forest which swarmed up steep, red hillsides, broken occasionally by white, Hispanic walls with iron gates in them, and the name of a villa spelled out in decorated tiles. Originality was clearly not the big thing here.

And then suddenly I was there. Two great stone columns supported a huge, steel gate, fifteen feet high and ten feet across. The walls were not so much walls as ramparts made of enormous blocks of solid granite. Above them grew cypress and thuja trees, dense, narrow and tall, pointing up to the blue sky. I followed the outer wall for a hundred yards or so, to where the road bore left and the wall turned right, in among the pinewoods.

I continued along the road to where it came to an abrupt end at the ruins of an old house. The place was covered in obscene graffiti and littered with trash and empty beer bottles. I parked, killed the engine and climbed out into the cool sunshine. There was a sign by the road that said this was a *mirador*, a place from which you could enjoy the view and take photographs. Especially recommended for those into trash and despair.

I did, however, have a fair view of Omeya's mansion, above me on my left. It was painted a kind of Mexican, adobe red, with corrugated tile roofs and a colonnaded terrace surrounded by those tall, narrow cypress trees. I couldn't see any people, and I wasn't all that keen for them to see me either.

So I climbed back in the Range Rover, switched on the camera and the laptop, and rolled slowly down the hill again. When I got to the big iron gate I stopped the truck and climbed out. I knew I was probably being watched on the villa's security cameras. So I made an elaborate show of opening the doors and closing them firmly, like the onboard computer was telling me something was open. I did the same with the trunk and then moved to the far side of the car where I was obscured from view. For the sake of completeness I opened and closed the doors there too. Then I hunkered down and clipped the camera carefully inside a young oak tree that was growing through the fence by the side of the road.

Finally, as I came back round to the driver's side I flipped a small, metal disk, about the size and shape of a coin or a washer, onto the sidewalk just outside the gate. Then I climbed inside the truck and checked the view from the camera on my computer. It was good enough to capture the license plate and the driver of whatever car was leaving the house. So I put the beast in gear and drove sedately back to the hotel, thinking about dinner. On the way I called Rentlux. A girl with a cute voice answered in English. Everybody in Marbella answers the phone in English. It's like Spanish is the second language there. She said what sounded like, "Nrrentaloox, ghow may I ghelp jou?"

I said, "Hi, this is Harry Reid. I'm renting a Range Rover from you right now. I'm going to need a Lamborghini Huracán convertible too, this afternoon."

"As gwell as the Range Rover, Mr. Reid?"

"Yeah."

She giggled softly and said, "That will be guan thousen' two hundred and forty-nine euros..."

"Can you deliver it to the *Puente Romano* this afternoon?"

"...per day."

"That's fine. Can you deliver it this afternoon?"

"Of course. I gwill personally make sure it is there in guan hours."

"Good. Leave the keys with reception."

I hung up and continued my sedate ride toward the gleaming Med. One thousand two hundred and forty-nine bucks a day. One thousand two hundred and fifty would have been extortionate, so they left it at forty-nine. What the hell! I told myself, if you're going to take out a billionaire, you gotta have the right ride.

Back at the hotel I put my laptop on the desk and fell on the bed, aiming to grab some of the sleep I had missed on the plane. I got little more than half an hour before my laptop pinged. I sat up, immediately awake, and moved to the desk.

On the screen I could see the steel door rolling back. I saw a lot of flowers, geraniums, bougainvillea, and a lot of flowerpots hanging from a wall that skirted a long, ascending driveway. Descending that ascending driveway was a bright red Ferrari 458 Italia. As it rolled over my small, metal washer I pressed F12, activating the magnet, and the metal disk jumped and attached itself to the underside of the chassis.

I opened the corresponding app on my cell and pretty soon I had her driving too fast down *Calle Montua* and onto the *Camino de Trapiche*. I had a quick shower, changed into my best billionaire playboy outfit and strolled down to reception to see if my Lamborghini had been delivered yet. It had, and was sitting outside getting some sun. I climbed in, put the soft-top down and made the engine growl like it was really mad about climate change and its impact on gender inequality. Then released that pent-up anger onto the Golden Mile, where I headed for Puerto Banus, smiling behind my six-hundred-dollar Armani shades, feeling like a million bucks.

I came off the A7 Mediterranean Freeway and growled my way onto the José Banús Avenue. There I rolled along under the palm trees that flanked the avenue and made a left onto a small, narrow, slightly shabby port. The road forked into a kind of right angle, embracing nine piers with about two hundred moored boats. There was everything from fiberglass two-seaters to small cruisers that looked more like spaceships than yachts. And lining the two prongs of the fork were the cafés and restaurants that offered you small tables, average food and drink and paper napkins at exorbitant prices, for the privilege of being able to say you were at Puerto Banus, and saw an anonymous Saudi prince drive past in his Ferrari.

I parked as conspicuously as I could and chose Patrick's Irish Pub over the A1 café. There I sat outside and ordered a Bushmills straight up, and while I was sipping it I checked my phone and saw that, as I had suspected, Rafaela Omeya was approaching in her 458.

My guess, relying on the fact that people do tend to conform to stereotypes, was that she would park near the Lamborghini, because it was a conspicuous sight, and would then go shopping at Dolce & Gabbana, on the far arm of the right angle.

Five minutes later the Ferrari rolled in and, sure enough, slid into the space two cars from mine. She climbed out and stood scanning the port for a moment, and I had to admit she was almost as good to look at as her car. The lights bleeped and she sashayed away along the *Muelle Salman*, toward Dolce & Gabbana. You have to love stereotypes.

I got to my feet and went after her. I paused along the way to look at absurdly expensive things, like glass vases, hunks of polished wood and mass-produced buddhas that nobody would want if they weren't absurdly expensive, and allowed her to pull ahead. Then I strolled on when I saw her push through the door into her favorite store.

Two got you twenty, I told myself, that she was buying shoes, though her main objective would be to have the shop staff fuss and fawn over her for half an hour. I strolled past, glanced in and had to smile. She was sitting on a stool with a middle-aged woman kneeling in front of her, slipping a shoe on her foot. I turned back and sat outside the La Lappardella, drinking an espresso and reading a local magazine all about people who lived in Marbella and shopped at places like Dolce & Gabbana: their loves, their dreams, their struggles and, above all, their money.

After thirty-five minutes she emerged from the shop holding a bag, and started walking back toward her car, typing a message on her phone.

FIVE

I dropped the paper on the table, stood and simultaneously pulled my phone from my pocket. Then, with perfect timing, I walked right into her, with considerable force, and knocked her bag and her phone right out of her hands. She staggered back and stood a moment staring at her things scattered on the ground. Her mouth was open and her eyes were wide. These things clearly don't happen to young lady billionaires. I felt I had somehow broadened her horizons and shown her possibilities she had never considered, like, people could bump into you and knock things out of your hands. Even if you were very rich.

I said, mildly, "I am so sorry."

She directed her astonishment at me as I bent to recover her things and muttered, "Here, let me help you."

"What is *wrong* with you?" Her accent was neutral American. I stood and handed her her bag and her phone.

"I wasn't looking where I was going. Like you. Are your things damaged? I'd be happy to replace them."

Her mouth worked hard on a "w" but couldn't decide whether to go with "what" or "why." Finally she said, "*I* wasn't looking where I was going? *You* collided with *me!*"

"No question, you're absolutely right. Will you please check your phone and your...," I peered at the paper bag, "Dolce & Gabbana shoes, to see if they are damaged?"

She frowned at me and I smiled. She was the center of attention and I was being nice to her, and I was pretty sure she wasn't going to let that go too quick. She sniffed and drew herself up with a show of dignity. Under the stupid act she was genuinely beautiful, and I thought for a moment it would be nice to see her relaxed and natural. She examined the phone and said severely, "The telephone is scratched. See? Here."

She pointed. I looked and nodded, though I couldn't see anything. Then she examined her shoes.

"They're OK. The box is dented. I like to keep the boxes. It's a *capricho*."

"Well," I said comfortably, "how can we fix this? First of all we can go to the store and get you a new box, and then we can either go together to an Apple store, or you can send me the bill at the Puente Romano."

She arched an eyebrow at me. "You don't even live here?"

I gave a laugh that was deliberately condescending. "Lord, no. I live in New York."

She was examining me now, shoes, watch, sunglasses. "What part?"

"Do you know New York? I'm in Manhattan, a stone's throw from the park. Look, I really feel bad about your phone. How can I make it up to you? Can we start with a drink?"

I gestured at the Italian restaurant I had just left. She hesitated a moment, then looked oddly defiant and said, "OK."

I noticed she hadn't smiled yet and told myself she was going to be hard work.

We moved back to the bar and sat. The waiter came hurrying out, bowing, smiling and rubbing his hands.

"*Señorita Omeya, que placer verla de nuevo!*" He turned to me then. "*Señor?*"

She didn't give me a chance to reply. She snapped, "*Champán!*" Then she made twiddley motions with her fingers over the table and added, "*Y nos pones unas gambitas.*" He bowed again and went away. She gave me that same, defiant look again and said, "I ordered champagne, and some prawns. You have a business card?"

I shook my head, affecting mild bewilderment.

"No. I have no business to have a card about."

"You have no business? So how..." She shrugged and spread her hands.

"Every now and then I go and see my brokers on Wall Street. They tell me what they are doing and how much I am making. I congratulate them on being real smart and then they take me out to lunch. If it's a really busy day they take me out to dinner instead. Do I need a card for that?" She blinked. I smiled some more. "I can give you my visiting card, if you like?"

She nodded and held out her hand. I handed her an embossed card with an address on the upper West Side, a little north of my own.

"Harry Reid," she said, looking at the card.

"Now you have to tell me your name."

"Rafaela. Rafaela Omeya." She stared hard at my face for a moment, like she was waiting for a reaction. When she didn't get one she relaxed a little. "My father has international business interests, but we live here."

I feigned a lack of interest and said, "So what are we going to do about your phone?"

She took it out and looked at the invisible scratch on the screen. For a moment I thought she was going to tell me to forget about it, which would have meant I'd have to work extra hard to see her again. But after a second she lifted her chin and said, "There's a shop in Marbella, near your hotel. We can go there and you can pay for it."

"Sounds good to me, Rafaela. Say, I'm here for a week, maybe more. I would love to get in a little skiing. And I've heard an awful lot about Spanish horses. I do a lot of riding on my ranch in Wyoming, but that's very different. We use the long stirrups and the loose reins."

She watched me in silence, with no expression. When I had finished she stared down at the table in front of her. The waiter brought a bucket of ice with a bottle of Mumm jammed in it and a couple of glasses. A waitress followed with some singed prawns. She kept staring at the table while the waiter poured and after he'd gone she sipped and finally looked at me.

"Are you trying to pick me up?"

"Not really." I shrugged. "You're pretty enough to try to pick up, but you're kind of serious. No, I was just trying to make conversation, and I'd like to do some skiing and riding while I'm here."

She was quiet again for a bit. It was starting to get on my nerves. But after a moment she said, "Water skiing is in summer. It is too cold now. Snow skiing is in Granada, Sierra Nevada."

"Oh, is that far?"

She almost smiled. "It depends what you are driving. If you are driving a BMW or a Mercedes, it can take maybe four hours. But if you are driving a Ferrari maybe you can do it in two hours."

My smile was smug, because I knew in that moment we were going to make a date to go skiing in Granada.

"How about if you're driving a Lamborghini?"

Now her lips curled just a little and touched her eyes with pleasure. "The Lamborghini is yours?"

"What Lamborghini?"

Now she giggled. I'd found her ticklish spot: lots and lots of money made her giggle. "Come on!" She pointed down the road, past the gleaming white yachts. "On the corner. Next to that beautiful red Ferrari."

"There's a Ferrari down there? I hadn't noticed."

Now she actually laughed. "You are bad! What do you mean, you didn't notice?"

"You'll have to show me. Maybe you could show me all the way to Granada."

She wagged a prawn at me. "*Pillo, pillo...*"

"Piyo piyo?" I asked.

"Nooo." She giggled. It's amazing the effect a Lamborghini can have on a spoilt brat. "The L is like the L in billiards. You have to make a little movement at the back of the tongue."

"Billiards, *pillo.*"

"It means bad boy."

"I do my worst. So, if I take you out to dinner, will you take me skiing?"

She ate the last prawn and drained her glass. I refilled it.

"Let me think about it, *pillin*. I don't know if I trust you."

"What's the worst I could do?"

Suddenly the humor drained out of her face and she reverted to pain-in-the-ass mode.

"I've got to go. You gave me your number. I'll call you."

I was going to ask what about her phone and her shoe box, but instead I said, "Sure. I'll be around for a week," and next thing she was strutting down the road toward her Ferrari.

I had long since given up trying to understand women. If Freud hadn't managed it, I sure as hell wasn't going to try. But this was dark by any standard. Had I overplayed my hand? Had I gone too far? Had I insulted her without realizing it?

I ate the last prawn and drained the last of the champagne, while trying to decide what to do next. Chances were if I ignored her she'd get in touch. She hadn't made any secret of the fact that she was a spoilt brat and she wanted to play with the kid with the Lamborghini. On the other hand, why the sudden change of mood? Why get up and march off without explanation?

I called the waiter and paid, then stood and made my way back to the car. The answer to my question was probably simply that she was basically narcissistic and wanted me to do exactly what I was doing: worrying about why she'd marched off the way she had. But, if she was going to let me down and not give me access to her father, then I needed a plan B.

Plan B was not going to be easy. The classic play would be to masquerade as an agent interested in buying arms. But my instinct was against it because Baldomero Omeya was not some Ivy League billionaire senator turned bad. He had been around the block so many times he'd made furrows in the sidewalk. He knew every play in the book, plus a few that hadn't even been written up yet. So a guy he'd never heard of, showing up out of left field and wanting to make a major purchase in weapons, would immediately alert him and probably get me killed. Especially if his charming daughter happened to see me and report our encounter.

I was either going to have to break in to his house, ninja style, and poison the bastard with curare, or drive him off the road and confirm the kill by breaking his neck. But in either of those cases, I also had to interrogate him before killing him. It was going to be anything but easy. I drove back toward the Puente Romano hotel, with the molten sun in my rearview mirror, declining in the west.

As it turned out, I needn't have worried so much. I pulled up at reception, tossed the keys of the Huracán to the kid from valet parking and, as I walked into reception, my phone pinged. I smiled to myself. I knew who it was so I didn't look at the message until after I had showered and changed my clothes.

The message was, as I had expected, from Rafaela. It said:

MR. REED, thank you, you were very kind to offer to have my phone mended. It is not necessary. As to skiing in Granada, I am sure your hotel will be able to arrange that for you. At risk of seeming discourteous, Mr. Reed, I must ask you please not to contact me again! Regretfully, Rafi

IT WAS ALL CAREFULLY TYPED out and correctly, if excessively, punctuated. It also gave me, apparently unintentionally, her phone number. I thought about sending her some kind of wiseass reply, but decided against it. She had decided she liked the *pillo*, so I figured I had better behave like one and ignore her.

I dined alone with my thoughts in the hotel restaurant, then retired early and got a good night's sleep.

SIX

THERE IS NOTHING PECULIAR OR WORRYING ABOUT A dark blue, or black Audi. There are thousands of them all over the world which belong to perfectly normal people. Equally, there is nothing especially odd about a dark blue Audi in a remote mountain parking lot in a national nature reserve, where families and schools go in order to feel they are getting to know nature.

But somehow, a dark blue Audi, in a remote parking lot in a remote nature reserve, becomes vaguely unsettling when occupied only by two men in their thirties who seem to have no particular purpose for being where they are.

The school bus was parked on a broad, dirt esplanade overlooking a broad vista of mountains covered in dense pinewoods. The place was called *Nacelrio,* which meant, roughly, "where the river is born," there was a beautiful wooded spring, and nearby a spectacular waterfall. So it was a popular place to bring kids at the end of term.

The kids were from two schools in Marbella. It was a joint outing before Christmas by Las Chapas, an all-girls school, and

Eco, an all-boys school, both owned by the Opus Dei. Maria de Los Angeles Martinez, who had turned nine in November, was with Las Chapas, and her brother, Luis, who had turned seven in June, was with Eco. Their father was an important man. He was General José Ferrer García, the supreme commander of all the *Guardia Civil* in Andalucia. But they had learned from a very early age not to talk about that to anyone.

There were thirty kids all told, the driver, two parent volunteers—sensitive, bearded fathers with senior posts in the local authority—and two teachers: Miguel and Juanita, whom everybody called *La Seño*.

The driver had sat in the bus, drunk his flask of coffee and eaten a cheese and ham roll while the teachers and the parents had led their kids through the forest to see where the stream sprang from the mountain and started its long, winding path, first to join with the *Cerezuelo* river, and then on down to the sea. The kids had collected samples of leaves, roots, moss and water, and then they had all trooped a quarter of a mile to where the spectacular waterfall cascaded among dappled light and foliage, over polished rocks and into a deeper, cold crystal channel. Here the kids had gathered more samples to be analyzed in school the next day.

After half an hour at the *Cascada de la Malena*, the teachers and the volunteer parents had led the children back along the trail through the woods to the broad expanse of the parking lot. There Miguel had spotted the two men leaning against the dark Audi, smoking. He was a broad-minded man with a beard, who listened to jazz and wore open-toed sandals in most weather, even when it was cold. So it was important to him not to make snap judgments about people. But even so, inside, he felt uncomfortable about the look of the men. There was a cold insolence in their eyes, and he couldn't escape the feeling that they watched the children with too much interest. He told himself they were probably waiting for their wives and children to return, and continued on his way to the bus, standing back and to the side a little to cluck at the children, with small plumes of condensation issuing from his mouth.

The Cap and Seth watched the children herded by and then watched them climbing on the bus in their warm woolen coats and hats, struggling to make the high steps as the clambered into the vehicle.

Once the last of them was onboard the Cap dropped his cigarette in the dirt, crushed it with his boot and crossed the lot to the bus, shouting, "Hold on there! *Espere por favor!* Wait up!"

He reached the door to see the driver frowning down at him. The Cap held up his hand and repeated, *"Espere, por favor,"* asking him to wait. The driver, an undercover sergeant from the *Guardia Civil*, shrugged and jerked his chin at him.

"Que pasa?" What's going on?

The Cap climbed the first couple of steps, smiling. It was an unpleasant smile. To Miguel, sitting just behind the driver, it was a smile that was full of menace. Seth climbed on behind the Cap and the driver started shaking his head.

"No, no. Privado. Autobús privado..."

And Miguel was on his sandaled feet, speaking limping English. "No, I am sorry. This is one bus private. It is school bus. You see," he gestured at the kids, "these are all schoolchildren."

He could see the almost wild amusement in the Cap's eyes, but he couldn't understand it. The Cap was nodding and behind him Seth was laughing. The Cap said, "Yeah, I can see it's a private bus, pal. But it is not a school bus anymore. No *autobus* for school."

La Seño asked Miguel, *"Que dice?"* What was he saying? The driver was getting to his feet. *"Get down the bus!"* Miguel ignored everyone and started to gesticulate a lot.

"No, you understand, this bus is for the school, Eco and Las Chapas. Is no for you come on."

The Cap became serious. "No, it's you who no understand, *amigo*. This bus is my bus now."

As he said it he smashed a right hook into Miguel's jaw. Miguel's legs turned to jelly and he fell in the aisle. There was a lot of screaming and, if the driver was about to act, he stopped when he found himself looking down the barrel of Seth's Glock 19. The Cap pulled his own Sig Sauer and waved it at *La Seño.*

"You," then he waved it at the two terrified parents, "and you, take him to the back."

They looked at him in blank horror. So he mimed lifting the unconscious teacher and dragging him back. Gingerly at first, but soon with a little more confidence, the three adults dragged the man toward the back of the bus, losing one sandal along the way. Seth waved the gun at the driver, who had his hands up and was sweating profusely over a waxy face.

"You," he said, in his grating, South African accent, "Git there, move!" He gestured at the place where Miguel had recently stood. As he slid into the aisle the Cap delivered the same right hook and the driver slumped on his back. The Cap looked at Juanita, *La Seño,* and arched his eyebrows. She and the two sensitive fathers dragged the driver back with the teacher. Seth climbed behind the wheel and started the engine. As he backed up and started to pull out of the parking lot, the Cap stood at the head of the aisle and spoke loudly and slowly.

"Does anybody here speak English? *Habla Ingles?*"

Some of the kids started to cry. Timidly one of the fathers raised a long, sensitive hand that had seen its fair share of typing.

"I am espik English a little." With finger and thumb he showed how little he spoke English. It was about half an inch. "I can translate, if you need."

The Cap grinned. "Good man. I need. What's your name, hombre?"

"I am Camilo. We are all espikin a little English."

"Yeah? OK, Camilo, I want you to translate what I am going to tell you. We are going to go real slow, so there is no mistake. OK?"

The bus made a big, broad turn onto the remote blacktop and they moved at a steady pace among the dense woodland, winding right and left along the hairpin bends. Camilo translated into Spanish. More kids started to cry. The Cap said:

"Nobody is going to get hurt."

Camilo translated.

"All you have to do is stay quiet, comfort the kids, do exactly as I say—"

Camilo spoke, making gestures of staying quiet and comforting the kids.

"And you can all go home this evening and be with your families."

An almost orgasmic expression of relief washed over Camilo's face as he translated the last bit. There was a burst of talking and crying and the Cap bellowed, "*Shut up! Silencio!*" There was quiet but for the stifled crying of the kids. He put his finger to his lips. "Quiet, and comfort the kids."

He stepped into the aisle and started walking down it, looking at the kids as he went, Finally he came to a girl with bright blonde hair and blue eyes who was hugging a boy of about six, with the same features. He smiled at her.

"Maria de Los Angeles Ferrer."

The little girl's bottom lip folded in and she began to cry.

"*Mi papa es un general, y le va a castigar por malo!*"

With the words "*papa*" and "*general*" he'd heard enough, but he raised his eyes to Camilo and jerked his chin. "She say she is daughter of one general, and he will punish you for being bad. She is just a child. She does not know..."

"Don't worry, Camilo. I am not going to hurt her. And this little boy is her brother, Luis, right?"

"Yes."

"Good, very good. Now, you," he pointed at *La Seño*, "comfort these kids and make them stop crying."

They had come to a stretch of road where the kids had been just a little earlier. On the right, instead of steep hills and forest, now the land dropped away dramatically into a deep gully maybe three hundred feet across, and maybe a hundred and forty feet deep, where the combined waters of the stream and the *Cerezuelo* crashed through a furious rapids toward the waterfall. Ahead a small esplanade appeared beside the road, barely big enough for the bus. From there it was a vertiginous drop to where the rapids gave way to the cascade.

Seth swung the wheel and inched onto the broad patch of dirt. There he put the bus in neutral and the Cap reached in his small rucksack and pulled out two mines. He showed them to the children, the parents and *La Seño*. Who stared back at him with slack jaws and wide eyes.

"OK, Camilo. These are mines, bombs, boom." Camilo started to translate, but the Cap kept talking. "I am putting one mine, *una bomba*, on the gas tank." He pointed toward where the gas tank was located on the bus. "*Gasolina*. And I am putting the other underneath the back of the bus." Again he pointed. "*Detras!* So if the mine explodes the bus goes in the river." He pointed and mimed elaborately. Everybody understood.

"Now explain this very carefully, Camilo. The mines are connected to motion sensors. If anybody tries to open the door, the mines will explode. If anybody tries to break the glass in the windows, the bombs will explode. If anybody tries to start the engine, the bombs will explode. The only thing you can do, is stay very still and wait for little Maria de Los Angeles' daddy to come and rescue you. Is that clear?"

He waited for Camilo to translate and explain. When he was sure they all understood, he took out his cell and made a call.

"Yeah, A-OK, make the call to the General José Ferrer García. We're all set here." He hung up, held up the phone and grinned at Camilo and at little Maria de Los Angeles. "*General José Ferrer García,*" he said. "*General José Ferrer García!*"

He saw the faint glimmer of hope in their eyes and laughed. Seth opened the doors and the Cap went to stand in the open doorway. Seth turned the bus so it was facing into the ravine, on a slight incline, and pressed the button to close the doors. The Cap, laughing, held them open and Seth scrambled from behind the wheel to jump out. The Cap jumped after him and they both heard the cacophony of screams as the bus lurched over the edge of the cliff and came to a grinding, precarious halt with its front wheel dangling in the air and the rear, just touching the ground, held down by the weight of the passengers. Seth placed the bomb, while the Cap gestured to the people inside to move to the back and remain motionless.

When the bus had stabilized he took photographs and Whats-Apped them to a secure number, where they would be forwarded to the General José Ferrer García, commander in chief of the Andalusian *Guardia Civil*.

SEVEN

I was at my table, contemplating the menu for lunch, when the receptionist peered into the dining room accompanied by a man in a blue suit. The receptionist pointed in my direction and the man in the blue suit crossed the room toward me with an expression on his face that said he hadn't had a good morning. I put down the menu and waited for him to arrive. His English was good, but heavily accented.

"Mr. Reid?"

"Yes."

"You will come with me, please."

I was genuinely surprised but covered it with a frown that was more curious than indignant.

"No."

He sighed and reached in his inside pocket. He handed me a badge in a leather folder.

"I am *Coronel Javier Sánchez Martínez,* of the *Guardia Civil.*"

I examined his badge and handed it back to him.

"Oh," I said simply and indicated the chair opposite mine. "Would you like to sit down?" He hesitated a moment. I pressed him, "Do you plan to arrest me for some reason?"

"No."

"Then why don't you join me, Colonel. We may as well talk over lunch as anywhere else."

His face said he could feel his authority draining away along with his control over the situation. But he harrumphed softly under his breath, pulled out the chair and sat. He drew breath to speak but I signaled the waiter and ordered two dry martinis, then said, "Colonel, how can I help you?"

"Yesterday you were meet with Rafaela Omeya in Puerto Banus."

I made a show of frowning and sitting back in my chair. It wasn't that much of a show. I was becoming more interested by the moment.

"I have several answers which spring to mind, Colonel, like, is that a crime? How the hell do you know? Are you spying on me? But I think I'm going to go with the simple, so what?"

We paused while the waiter handed us our drinks and I told him I wanted a sirloin steak with salad. The colonel watched me from under his eyebrows. When the waiter had gone away he said, "You admit that you met with her?"

I knew there was no point denying it, but I was curious whether he knew I'd met her because he had been following me or her. So I said, "Bullshit," and added, "I don't *admit* any damned thing. I'm not under arrest, I am not under oath in court and I am not accused of anything. You say I met Rafaela somebody-or-other in Puerto Banus yesterday. Maybe I did and maybe I didn't. And before I tell you a god-damned-thing, you had better tell me why you're asking me."

I guess colonels in the *Guardia Civil* don't often get spoken to that way. Anger made his eyes shiny and suppressed rage turned his olive skin a kind of unhealthy gray. He licked his lips and took a sip of his martini before replying.

"I would advise you, Mr. Reid, to take a different tone with officers of the law in this country."

I smiled blandly. "Thanks for the advice. I'll pass it on to my lawyers in case they ever sue the Spanish government. Now would you mind telling me exactly why you are asking about what I did yesterday? And while you're at it, you had better have a damned good explanation for why you are spying on me."

"Do not flatter yourself, Mr. Reid. We are not spying on you. My men were conducting a surveillance operation and saw you meet with *Señorita* Omeya."

"A surveillance operation on whom?" I asked, thinking the brigadier would be proud of my use of the object pronoun.

"I am not going to discuss *Guardia Civil* investigations with you, Mr. Reid. I have told you we were not watching you. Now, will you please explain to me why you met with Rafaela Omeya?"

I sipped my martini and thought about it. I arched an eyebrow at him.

"Is she involved in some kind of illegal activity?"

He sighed again. "Mr. Reid, are you involved in any activity that will be of interest to the Spanish *Guardia Civil*?"

I made a "that's all I damn well need" face and snapped, "No, of course not!"

"Then, if we are not interested in you, I invite you to draw your own conclusions as to why I am asking you about Rafaela Omeya. Now, will you please answer my question?"

I grunted and the waiter brought me my steak and a glass of Rioja. I spoke as I cut into the meat.

"My meeting with Rafaela was totally fortuitous. I was having coffee at a bar. I stood, checking the messages on my phone, and walked right into her. That's about all there is to it."

He did that thing Mediterraneans do, where they hunch their shoulders, spread their hands and arch their eyebrows. It seems to say, *What are you talking about? Isn't it obvious?* and *Are you blind?* all in one simple gesture. What he said was, "Buah! But you had lunch! Prawns, champagne..."

I smiled on the most annoying side of my face. "You should try looking at her as a woman instead of a suspect for a couple of minutes. If you bumped into all that, wouldn't you offer to buy her lunch?"

"Mr. Reid, please..."

"I made her drop her phone and her new shoes. I offered to pay for the damage. She was cagey, so I offered her a drink. She decided prawns and champagne would be better than a drink."

"You agreed to meet again?"

I shrugged. "I tried, but she wasn't interested."

"You have heard from her again?"

I shook my head. "Not since she told me she didn't want to see me anymore."

He didn't look particularly happy or convinced, but he nodded.

"Mr. Reid, please, allow me to give you some advices. Rafaela Omeya may be a very beautiful woman. But there are many beautiful women in Spain. This one can bring you many problems. It is best that you do not make any more contacts with her."

"Thank you, Colonel. I'll bear it in mind."

He went to stand, but sucked his teeth a moment and sat again.

"What is your reason for visiting Spain, Mr. Reid?"

"Pleasure, Colonel. Hemingway, Orson Welles, there are a number of famous Americans who loved this part of the world."

He nodded. "Both of those men went to Ronda, not Marbella. Perhaps you should do the same."

"Oldest bullring in Spain. It's on my list."

He stood. "Thank you for the drink, Mr. Reid." He shrugged one shoulder and looked thoughtful for just a moment. "I hope we do not meet again."

I was going to tell him the feeling was mutual, but I thought I might hurt his feelings. So I gave a no-hard-feelings laugh and watched him cross the dining room back toward the lobby.

So the *Guardia Civil* were watching Rafaela. I wondered if they were watching her in her own right, or if it was just an extension of a broader, routine watch that they kept on her father.

Either way it could be a problem if I was going to use her to get close to Baldomero.

A little more thought while I ate my steak and sipped my wine told me it was unlikely they had plainclothes colonels dropping in on everyone she made contact with. But then they probably already knew the people she usually made contact with. Now here, out of the blue, is an American who hires luxury cars like they come free with cornflakes, and happens to bump into her in Puerto Banus. That would draw closer interest.

If I didn't meet with her again they'd probably let it slide. But if I did, they'd start watching me like hawks. I was back where I had been when I thought I'd blown it with Rafaela: I had plan A, and plan B would require about six months to set up if it was to have the remotest chance of success. My only chance was to stick with plan A, use Rafaela, get the job done fast and move out before the *Guardias* had a chance to react.

I took out my cell and glanced at it, thinking. She had remained silent since her message last night. I knew that message, despite what it said, was a prelude to closer contact. She was as suspicious of me as the *Guardias* were, maybe more so, and she was playing cautious trying to find out what I was about. And both that, and the visit from the colonel, begged the questions, how deep was Rafaela in her father's business? And, how much information could I get from her?

I drummed my fingers on the table, wondering whether to call her, but knowing that every minute I delayed, every minute I maintained my indifference, was another ounce of advantage in my favor.

I rose and made my way to the reception, weighing what my next step should be. That was when my phone rang. It was the brigadier.

"Hello, darling? How nice to hear from you. Are you in Marbella?"

"Get to a television and turn on the Spanish news."

I glanced around, saw a small salon with a TV in it and made my way inside. As I sat in an armchair I asked, "What am I looking for?"

"It will be breaking news. Find it and call me when you've acquainted yourself with the facts."

He'd hung up by the time I managed to tell him that my Spanish was good enough to ask if somebody spoke English. But pretty soon I had found a news channel and figured out that the breaking story was about a busload of kids which had crashed in the mountains in Jaen, a province north of Malaga. From what I could make out, watching the footage taken from a circling helicopter, the coach was balanced on the edge of a precipice over a deep gorge, with a river running through the bottom. Beside the gorge was a snaking road that ran through a sprawling pine forest. I could see basic emergency services parked nearby, but nobody seemed to want to touch the bus. They were probably scared it might go over.

As the chopper proceeded, circling the area, I could make out a couple of military green *Guardia Civil* Land Rovers blocking access from the road. There was also an ambulance and a fire truck, neither of which would be of any use if the worst happened. I figured they'd probably just sent everyone and anyone they had handy, and in a remote place like that, the fire truck and the ambulance was probably about it.

"Damn thing's got a bloody tow bar..."

I looked up. There was a guy with white hair, cream pants, a dark blue blazer and a silk cravat tucked into a pale blue shirt. He was leaning on the doorjamb holding a gin and tonic in his hand.

"It has a tow bar?" I repeated as a question.

He pointed at the TV. "The bus. Seen it a couple of times already. Every time the camera closes in...see? There it is! Look! Bloody tow bar!"

I looked. The camera had closed in on the scene and, at the angle the bus was perched, you could see very clearly a tow bar sticking out the back.

"I'll be damned," I said.

"Olive-growing land, up there in Jaen. Must be hundreds of bloody tractors all over the bloody place. Sling a chain on the damn thing and pull it out. Look at all the space they've got! A child could do it. Bloody Spaniards! Hopeless. No idea of engineering. Can't get anything right." He looked at me and grinned. "Make a damned fine G and T though."

I gave him the best laugh I could muster. "You got that right." Then I turned back to the screen.

The man was not wrong. It was on a large esplanade, a broad area of dirt beside the road, like an improvised parking lot. The bus had obviously pulled in there for some reason and in turning around it had come off, though it was hard to imagine how the driver had managed to do that, unless he was drunk. But all they needed to do now was hitch the tow bar to a tractor with a steel rope, or a chain, and haul it out. There was plenty of room for the maneuver. It should be simple to do. I turned back to the guy in the cravat. "My Spanish isn't great. What are they saying?"

"Bunch of schoolkids, Christmas outing. Some exclusive school from Marbella. Oh..." He paused and nodded. "Two schools, Eco and Las Chapas, boys and girls respectively. Very expensive private schools run by the Opus Dei, big thing here. Obviously had a joint Christmas outing to go and see the nature reserve up there in Cazorla. Biggest in Europe, bears, wolves, golden eagles..."

"So that bus is full of Marbella's most privileged kids?"

"Privileged Spanish kids, yes. Brits and Scandies, we tend to have our own schools. But that coach must be carrying all sorts of important people's children. Heads will roll, no doubt." He laughed, like it was funny. "And now, for some reason best known to themselves, they're not letting the reporters anywhere near the place. One bugger with a telephoto lens is saying there is no sign of the driver. He's spotted the teachers and two parents, but no sign of the driver. No doubt they'll be dreaming up some conspiracy theory before long."

I was still thinking about what he'd said before. "Opus Dei?"

"Eh? What? Oh, the school, yes. They own all the most exclusive schools in Spain. Very powerful mafia. You send your kids to their schools and they're made for life." He looked into his drink. "I suppose the poor sod had a stroke or something, and collapsed. That's why he went over the edge."

"That's probably what happened," I said, watching a dark Mercedes pull up at the scene, and the green Land Rover pull back to let it through.

"There'll be some very important people worrying about their kids tonight, though."

"There will at that," I said. "Thanks for interpreting."

"Pleasure, old chap."

I made my way out of the hotel and onto the Boulevard Principe Alfonso von Hohenlohe, which I guessed somebody, somewhere, once upon a time, must have been able to pronounce. I called the brigadier.

"You got the gist?"

"Hi darling, yes, and how are you?"

"Where are you?"

"Strolling down the Boulevard Prince Alfonse von Hohenlohe. All those Hs and all of them silent. It seems such a waste."

"There is no risk of being overheard?"

"None at all, sweetheart."

"Then you can cut the crap, Harry. The children in that bus..."

"I'm guessing they're hostages."

"Probably. We checked the schools—"

"Two of them, Eco and Las Chapas. They both belong to the Opus Dei."

He was silent for a second. "Correct. Curiously enough Eco was the school attended by Omeya's stepbrother. Among the children there are two who are particularly high-value targets, Maria de Los Angeles Martinez and her brother, Luis. They are nine and seven, respectively."

"Who's their father?"

"General José Ferrer García, the supreme commander of the *Guardia Civil* in Andalusia."

"Bingo. And therefore responsible for anti-terrorism and security at the ports of Algeciras, Cadiz and Malaga."

"Precisely."

"So that's why they're not towing the bus."

There was a frown in his voice. "What?"

"The bus, it has a tow bar. It would be simple to attach a steel rope to the tow bar and pull it back with a couple of tractors. But they're not doing it, because there's a bomb on the bus."

He sounded astonished. "You know that?"

"I'm putting two and two together and making four."

"I see. Well, yes, that does seem likely."

"According to your analysis, the goods Omeya took from Groom Lake must be due to arrive in Cadiz, Algeciras or Malaga in the next couple of days. He needs insurance that the goods are not going to be held at customs. So he takes the commander of the *Guardia Civil*'s kids hostage until the goods are through."

"That seems a fair assessment."

"So what are you telling me to do?"

"We have to abort, Harry. We make one wrong move and the blood of those children is on our hands."

"And that bastard gets away with it again."

"We can come back. We are postponing, not canceling."

"And what is our guarantee that he won't kill the kids anyway? And how do we know that the next time we come after him, he won't have another school or another orphanage dangling on a string? This bastard likes going after kids."

"We don't know, Harry, but we can't put these children's lives at risk. You know that."

"Yeah," I said. "I know that." He was about to hang up but I stopped him. "Sir?"

"Yes, Harry?"

"So I am back on vacation, right?"

"Yes, I suppose you are. Why?"

"I always thought Hemingway was overrated, but I always liked Orson Welles. They both spent a lot of time in Ronda—"

"Welles's ashes are buried there, in a well on a ranch, *El Recreo De San Cayetano* ranch, on the A367. I've been there a couple of times."

"Exactly, I knew that," I lied. "I thought I might take a few days and go check it out."

There was a long silence, then, "Harry, there are thirty children on that bus. Do not do anything, *anything,* that might put them at risk."

"I wouldn't do that, sir."

"No," he said, like he was reassuring himself. "No, I don't believe you would."

EIGHT

I STOOD A WHILE LEANING AGAINST A WHITEWASHED wall beside a big brassy bunch of bougainvillea, watching the Marbella traffic slide past in the inappropriately warm December sun. My eyes took in the cars, with the occasional Ferrari and Bentley, but my mind was seeing something else.

My mind was seeing a container truck driving through the night from Nevada toward Virginia, passing through Utah and Colorado. I was seeing one of the most trusted, effective special ops teams in Delta being taken out and the truck hijacked. If I were in charge of that operation, what would I do with that container?

The answer wasn't hard. Your first priority, having taken possession of the container, would be to get rid of it as fast as you could. And that would mean getting it out of the USA as fast as possible. Taking it back west to ship across the Pacific didn't make a lot of sense. It would be an unnecessary waste of time. The simplest option was to continue east and ship to either Latin America, Africa or Europe.

If the brigadier was right and this was the work of Baldomero Omeya, then it would make sense that he was selling either to the

Chinese or the Russians. They were the USA's biggest competitors, and about the only players with the kind of budget that could buy straight off the Groom Lake drawing board. The quickest route to both Russia and China was through the Mediterranean. China would then be right, through the Suez Canal, and Russia would be left, through Istanbul and the Black Sea. And the first port of call on arriving in Europe, after crossing the Atlantic, would be either Cadiz or Algeciras.

I pushed off the wall and made my way back toward the hotel. Cadiz was a couple of hours away and I figured I could do worse than go and snoop around there for a while—after I'd dropped into the *Corte Inglés* superstore for some essential hardware.

THE LANDSCAPES along the Mediterranean coast of Malaga are reminiscent of the Trans-Pecos region of Texas, or Arizona if it had a coastline. It's a dramatic mix of arid and green, with craggy peaks and tables that stand out against the sheer blue sky. But I wasn't looking at the landscapes. I wasn't even paying much attention to the dark blue Audi that had been a hundred and fifty yards behind me since San Diego. My mind was on the thirty children confined in the back of the bus, teetering over the gorge in Cazorla.

At San Roque I turned into the Bay of Gibraltar and spent an hour nosing around the bars and the various shipping companies on the port. I didn't learn anything interesting there and eventually climbed in the Range Rover and took the N340 seventy miles along the Atlantic coast of Spain to Cadiz.

Cadiz is a small island that lies less than a mile off the coast, and is connected to it by an artificial spit of land and two bridges. The port takes up a large chunk of the northeastern side of the island and covers an area of about eight hundred and twenty-five acres, which is about one third the total area of the island. It's an important port in Spain, where Sir Francis Drake, in 1587, famously entered and sank most of the Spanish fleet where it sat moored at the docks, and departed laughing that he had singed the King of Spain's beard.

A stroll around the area revealed a medium-sized container ship with a Spanish courtesy flag and an American ensign. The name stenciled on the prow was the *Princess Diana*. The ensign told me she was an American ship, but little else.

Enquiries at the port office and the local bars revealed only that the ship had just docked within the last few hours. Inquiries about the captain and the crew managed to irritate the port official, but elicited no more information of any interest, except that it was to be unloaded in the next day or so.

Feeling vaguely like I had wasted the afternoon, and telling myself I wasn't a damned detective or a spy, I called the brigadier and told him what little I had learned. He listened in silence before saying, "I thought you were on vacation."

"I am, they have great seafood in Cadiz."

"Leave it alone, Harry."

"You're welcome."

I hung up and headed back toward Marbella in the growing dark, driving against the thick stream of headlamps flowing the other way on the far side of the barrier.

I pulled in at the hotel just before nine PM, went to my room and had a shower while I wondered what to do next. I let the scalding water pound my head and face, then switched it to cold to see if it would wake up my neurons. Then switched back and forth a couple more times. But when I stepped out of the shower I still had no idea what to do. What I couldn't do was crystal clear. I could not interfere, and I could not put the kids at risk, and neither could I walk away. It was a double bind.

I toweled my hair dry and shaved—with soap and a razor, the way men do—and splashed aftershave on my face. It stung, but I still couldn't get past the double bind.

I pulled on my pants and there was a knock at the door. A

rapid process of elimination told me who it was. So I opened it without putting on my shirt. I noticed for the first time that she was short, maybe five-three or four. I noticed also she was in flat sandals and she had pretty feet. One of them had a tattoo in what looked like Sanskrit. The rest of her was draped in a very fine, violet cotton dress that made you want to take a hold of her and squeeze. She was looking at me from under her eyebrows in a way that managed to suggest submission. Behind her, lamplight touched the cobbles of a small bridge over a small stream. For some reason that didn't help much.

I looked at her a while without saying anything, then arched an eyebrow.

"Yes?"

"You have every right to be angry with me."

"I have? Why's that?"

"Harry," she said softly, "you are being unkind."

I gave a small laugh which was meant to sound ironic. "I'm being unkind? What was it you wanted, Miss Omeya?"

She looked down at her hands and slowly rubbed the back of her thumbnail.

"I came to apologize. But you are not making it very easy."

"Let me see, I apologized for making a microscopic scratch on your telephone and denting your shoebox, I invited you to a luncheon of champagne and king prawns and asked you about skiing. I missed the bit where I was so grotesquely rude you had no choice but to send me a message forged in the Antarctic telling me not to contact you anymore. So maybe you can give me one reason why I should make it easy."

I thought I had nailed the petulant millionaire playboy who has been turned down in spite of driving a Lamborghini. By the way her eyes searched my face, I figured she thought so too.

"That hurt," she said at last. "I do not like to be cold, but I have learned that I must be. Will you invite me in?"

I sighed and stepped back, holding the door open for her. She came in and I closed it behind her. She was close, just a few inches away, looking up into my face. I brushed past her, went into the bedroom and pulled a shirt from the wardrobe.

"What's this about, Rafaela?"

She didn't answer until I turned to look at her. She was standing in the bedroom door with one hand on the jamb. I shrugged on the shirt and waited.

"I wanted to explain. I felt..." She hesitated. "I felt you were different."

I shook my head, telling her it wouldn't wash. "Different to what?"

Her voice was barely a whisper. "To other men."

"Bullshit."

"Maybe I was wrong..."

The sadness on her face looked genuine. I sighed and went and leaned on the door, looking down at her.

"OK, I'm sorry. I guess nobody likes being rejected, and your rejection was pretty cold." I shrugged like I was fifteen and added, "And I guess I liked you."

She raised her face and said, quickly, "Did you? I liked you too."

"Then why the message?"

Again she looked down at her thumbs. "It's complicated."

"Husband complicated or boyfriend complicated?" I asked, like it made a difference.

She turned abruptly and walked away, toward the sofa. When she got there she stood staring out of the black window behind it. I said:

"If you're married you shouldn't be here."

She sat slowly, carefully, like she might break something if she sat too fast.

"I'm here because I am married."

"Then you'd better—"

"Please! Stop talking. Just listen to me."

For a moment I did nothing. Then I ran my fingers through my hair and asked her,

"You want a drink?

She nodded. "Gin and tonic. I feel…"

She didn't finish the sentence. I mixed her drink, handed it to her and poured myself a scotch.

"What? You feel what?"

"Nervous."

I sat in an armchair and crossed one leg over the other.

"You're married, your father has a reputation to think about and you're here in my hotel room apologizing for a message you sent telling me not to contact you anymore. I'd say you have good reason to be nervous. What the hell is this about, Rafaela?"

"My father…" She covered her face with her hands for a moment. "You are going to think I am crazy. My father is not my father, he is my husband."

"Baldomero Omeya is your husband."

"Yes."

"Why the hell did you tell me he was your father?"

"He is forty years older than me. He is one of the most powerful men in Spain. Anything he wants, he has. He met me and decided he wanted me. He bought my parents a beautiful house with a pool, near the sea. He bought my father a Mercedes, my brother he sent to university in *Santiago de Compostela*, and never asked for anything from me… Until my whole family was dependent on him. Then he told me, marry me or they will all be living on the streets in a week."

"So you married him."

"Of course I did. What else could I do? He gives me every-thing I want, and I take everything I can." She picked up her glass and examined it for a few seconds, then said savagely, "But the shame! I am young! Beautiful! With that fat, ugly, cruel man! So when I go out, always on my own, I tell people he is my father. And then they respect me. But inside I live with this feeling. I am a slave, and I disgust myself."

She studied my face for a reaction but didn't find any. She sighed and went on.

"He wants a son. Not a child, not to love and fulfill his family. He wants a son to immortalize himself at the head of his empire. And that means that once every month I must perform my conjugal duties."

"That's tough."

"Tough? It is rape. He takes his pill, he comes to my room. I do as I am told, and he leaves when he is finished. He has started to complain that I am barren, that I am not a real woman…"

"But you are secretly using a contraceptive."

She nodded. "I will not have that bastard's child. I would rather tear out my *matriz* than carry his child!"

There were no prizes for guessing that a *matriz* was a womb. It was all very passionate and Spanish, and I wasn't sure whether to believe it or not. I sipped, savored and swallowed while I studied her face. The cold haughtiness she had displayed at Puerto Banus was gone. In its place was a frightened, angry young woman who was full of passion and warmth.

"Why are you telling me all this?"

"I—" She drew breath as though a torrent of words was about to spill out. But she closed her eyes and her mouth and sagged back into the sofa. "I don't know," she said at last. "I am a silly girl. I thought you liked me." She opened her eyes but looked at her glass instead of me. "I thought maybe if we talked you could help me."

"Help you to do what?"

She shook her head again and made to stand. "I have been stupid. I should go."

"Sit down, will you. I didn't say I wouldn't help you. But if I am going to help you I need to know what I am helping you to do, right?"

She stared at me for a long moment. "You would help me?"

"That depends, Rafaela, on what you want help with." We sat in silence, staring at each other. I pressed her. "You want help getting out of that marriage, I'll help you. You want help with your parents, we'll see what we can do. You want help killing Omeya..."

I let the words linger, studying her face. There was excitement in her eyes, the threat of a smile at the corners of her mouth. I grinned.

"I don't do that kind of thing."

She sat forward suddenly. "I just want a normal life! To be free from *him*, and my family to be safe. But I know, if I try to leave him, he will destroy us all."

"I think I should meet him. Why don't you introduce us?"

"Impossible! Nobody comes close to him."

"I'm pretty sure we could think of something."

"He does not scare you?"

I smiled. "Not so far."

"If he dislikes you, or is angry with you, he can hurt you. He is dangerous, Harry."

"I believe you."

She set her glass on the table in front of her and came to kneel on the sheepskin rug in front of me. She placed her hands on my knee and pressed her body against my leg.

"Harry, I am twenty-three years old. For three years I have not felt like a woman. For three years I have not been with a man. I have been only with that monster."

"Your husband."

"He is not my husband. He is my master, my owner, but not my husband. To marry someone you must make promises with your heart, with your soul. Not out of fear. Do you believe that?"

"Yes."

"Harry, help me."

She got to her feet suddenly and crossed the floor behind me to the bedroom door. I heard her voice, almost a whisper, "Harry, look at me..."

I stood and turned, and saw her light dress drop softly, silently to the floor. All she had on was a pair of violet, lace panties and a lace bra of the same color. Against her olive skin it looked stunning. When she spoke, it was a genuine plea, with real sadness in her eyes.

"Please, Harry, make me feel like a woman again."

I put down my whisky, picked her up in my arms and carried her to the bed.

NINE

12:20 PM THURSDAY 12-09-2021, CAZORLA, SOUTHERN SPAIN

SHE WAS STILL ASLEEP WHEN I HAD RISEN AT FIVE thirty the next morning. I'd had a cold shower and called room service for coffee while I dressed. By five fifty-five I was out on the road, headed north and east through the dark, among the desolate streetlamps, toward the province of Jaen, high in the Andalusian mountains.

It took me a little over three hours to get to the small, picturesque town of Cazorla. The landscapes on the way are said to be some of the most dramatic and beautiful in Spain, but I didn't get to see them. Dawn was breaking at eight thirty, just as I was pulling into the town square. I parked opposite the bar *Cura Tapas* and had four espressos and a toasted roll.

As I finished my breakfast I could see the sun dancing on the fountain in the center of the square, and people, huddled into coats and hats, beginning to mill. I called for the check. As I was paying I asked, in halting Spanish, where the bus was with the trapped kids. Turned out, like most Spaniards, he spoke halting English better than I spoke halting Spanish.

He said something that sounded like, "Bamohabé!" Which I later found out was "*vamos a ver*"—let's see. "Bamohabé, *usted*, you, you takin' de road *Camino del Sol*, is very bad road. Is goin' up an' up an' up—" He swayed from foot to foot, elevating his hands as he did so. "Up an' up, when you comin' to a fock in the road. An' you are takin' the left fock and goin' up an' up an' up, to *Hermita San Sebastian*. Very nice, you look!" He stuck out his hand in front of him and opened his eyes wide in astonishment. "Oooh! Wonderful! Beautiful. Then you keep on! Up, up, up. An' when you are up top, you see too many police. *Guardia Civil* everywhere. Then," he nodded a lot with his whole body, "then, this is bus here."

I gave him a buck for the advice and the performance and went out to climb in the Range Rover. I followed his instructions, which were remarkably accurate, and made my way "up an' up an' up," winding through very dense pine forests on hairpin bends that were close to three hundred and sixty degrees, and a gradient that must have been fifteen or sixteen degrees, and at times steeper.

I climbed for maybe twenty or twenty-five minutes, with the trees arching over the road and forming long, dappled green tunnels that were broken by sudden outcrops of rocks and boulders. Until finally I came to a sharp right-hand turn and saw, up ahead, a green, military Land Rover, a mobile barrier and two *Guardia Civil* with assault rifles hung across their chests.

I rolled up not too fast and not too slow and one of the cops held up his hand, telling me to stop. I did, and leaned out the window. He was a young guy in his early thirties, dressed in camouflage fatigues. He was wagging his finger in the negative, "*Paso prohibido! De la vuelta!*" And he gestured with the same finger I had to turn around and leave.

I called to him as he approached, "*Por favor, Nacelrio?* Do you speak English? I want to go to *Nacelrio!*"

"No! Is cut. The road is cut. You go back. Is prohibit pass. *Paso prohibido!* You go back!"

He didn't look like he wanted to get into a conversation about it. So I gave him the thumbs up, did a three-point turn and headed slowly back down the mountainside.

After about ten minutes I came to the hermitage the waiter had mentioned in the bar. It was on a sharp rise between two deep gullies, skirted by the road. It was disused and crumbling, and behind and beyond it was dense, wild forest.

I pulled off the road and rolled and jolted my way across the rocks and potholes until I came to the crumbling, stone building. I found a place to park that wasn't too visible from the road, killed the engine and swung down from the cab. I pulled my new hardware, which I had bought from the *Corte Inglés* superstore, from the trunk and started to make my way up into the woodlands. The hill was steep and the going was tough. At times I needed to grab onto the trees to haul myself up, but that was fine by me. The harder the place was to get to, the less likely I was to be disturbed.

After about half an hour of scrambling and climbing, I eventually broke out of the trees and found myself just below an arid peak. Ahead of me the hill climbed, almost vertically, among brush and small bushes, to a cluster of boulders that loomed against the blue sky.

I turned and looked back along the way I had come. The tall, dense pines made a thick, dark wall with an even denser, green canopy, swooping down steeply into the valley below, where the town of Cazorla sprawled. And beneath me, over to my left, I could see perfectly the site where the bus had been stranded.

It was about half a mile, or three-quarters of a mile away, a rocky bluff overlooking a deep gorge that was overgrown with bushes and trees that clung to the ledges with roots like claws. The bluff looked like it had been flattened on top, but was dirt rather than asphalt. I could make out the bus, suspended with its front wheels dangling over the precipice and its rear wheels three or four feet up in the air. It struck me that if they had a storm, or a strong wind, they'd have a real problem on their hands.

There was one green Land Rover visible and a couple of men in green uniforms standing around looking useless. Aside from that I could not make out any more details. The trees and the rocks effectively cut it off from view.

I found a comfortable place to sit where I would not be visible from the rocky bluff and unpacked my new hardware. It had cost me three grand, but the DJI Mavic 3 drone had a high-resolution, professional Hasselblad camera and could stay airborne for three-quarters of an hour, while feeding live video over a range of up to seven miles.

There wasn't much wind, but what there was, was coming from the northwest, across the valley. So I got the drone up in the air and climbed to about three thousand feet, where the drone was a silent speck against the sky. Then I swung it around to approach the site from the southeast, so the wind would carry away what little noise the props made. The thick canopy of the pines made it invisible from the road.

I closed in slow, doing about twenty miles per hour, slowed right down to a hover, staying high, and surveyed the area. I could see the bus clearly. Its angle over the gorge was more acute than I had thought, and keeping everyone, especially the kids, cramped in the back on a sloping floor must have been exhausting.

There were two *Guardia Civil* Land Rovers on site, a crane and a couple of tractors. Zooming in with the camera I could confirm that the bus did have a tow bar, like the guy at the hotel had said. With the horsepower and weight they had down there, they could have pulled the coach clear hours ago. If they weren't touching it, it was because they were scared. And the only thing that I could think of that could scare them off moving the bus, was a bomb. But that was something I had to confirm as a certainty, and for that I needed to have a look under the chassis.

I knew if I got in too close the cops would see the drone, and there was an outside chance they might try to track it back to its owner. In the end I figured it was a chance I was going to have to take. So I pulled over to the north and dropped into a steep dive into the gorge and swept up under the front of the bus, quick-firing pictures as I went. I shot up a thousand feet, turned and dived again, doing fifty miles an hour as I hurtled toward the ground. I could see the cops pointing. One of them raised his rifle but he couldn't shoot in case he hit the bus. I skimmed the ground, scanned the underside and hurtled up again on the far side, taking one last look at the gas tank inlet. Then I shot up to the drone's ceiling, at twenty thousand feet, where it became invisible, and reeled it in.

With the drone packed safely in its box I scrambled my way slowly back down through the forest. I'd taken plenty of pictures, and I would review them carefully once I was back at the hotel, but the crucial thing was that I had seen the bombs. There were two of them: one on the gas tank and the other under the rear axle, set to blow the bus into the ravine in a ball of flames if anybody tried to move it. With everybody crammed in the back, right over the gas tank, they didn't stand a chance. And two got you twenty the damned things were detonated by motion sensors, so there would be no way to remove them unless the detonators were deactivated.

I got back to the truck, slung the drone in the trunk and climbed behind the wheel. I had taken the job. When the brigadier had aborted I had known I would not stop. I would keep going. He had known it too. But now, having seen what Omeya had done with the bus, with thirty children in the back, a breeze away from a death too ghastly to imagine—having seen all that, I knew I was going to kill him. I knew it as an absolute fact.

When I got back to the Puente Romano hotel, I sent the pictures to the brigadier. Then I checked on my laptop and saw that Rafaela's Ferrari was in Benalmadena, about twenty minutes away. She was parked outside the Buddhist Stupa. Somehow that didn't surprise me as much as it might have. I thought about it for all of fifteen seconds, then called the brigadier. He didn't let me speak.

"Harry, you are worrying me. Please, go back to Wyoming and spend a couple of weeks hunting deer."

"Yes, sir. Have you looked at the photographs?"

"Yes. You should not have gone there."

"I know. Sir, you've seen there are two limpet mines, one on the gas tank, the other under the rear axle. When they blow they will ignite the gas in the gas tank and all the people—all those kids we are worrying about—who right now are crammed into the back of the bus as a counterweight, right over the gas tank, will be engulfed in a ball of fire. They don't stand a chance. My guess is the mines are detonated by motion sensors. So there is no way to remove them unless the detonators are deactivated."

He sounded tired when he sighed. "Yes, Harry. I am having the pictures analyzed as we speak. But I would say you are almost certainly correct."

"So we need to know if an EMP will kill the detonators. But I am guessing there will be a failsafe of some kind. I thought about a human agent with some kind of remote control, but an EMP would kill that too. I can't figure what the failsafe would be."

"No doubt our analysts will know. Harry?"

"Yes sir?"

"Go to Wyoming."

"Yes sir. I am booking the tickets as we speak. On a separate issue, have you any operatives in Malaga? Or can we borrow a couple from the Company?"

He was quiet for five long seconds before answering. "I might be able to borrow a couple. The Company has a field office in Malaga. What's on your mind?"

I told him what was on my mind and he thought about it for ten even longer seconds (Count them out. It's a long time). Finally he said, "All right, Harry. But if a single one of those children dies, it's on your head."

"Yeah, I am aware of that, sir. This has to be quick and it has to look real."

"How long will you take to get there?"

"Half an hour."

"All right. I'll make the call."

I hung up and called reception to have the Hurracán ready for me. Five minutes later I was surging onto the toll road, burning rubber toward Benalmadena at a hundred and forty miles an hour. Spanish roads, especially on the south coast, are not German autobahns, and the drive came pretty close to being a terrifying experience. But I needed to get to the Buddhist Stupa before Rafaela suddenly decided she needed a new pair of Prada shoes. I needed to get to her fast.

It took me all of twelve minutes to cover the entire twenty-five miles from the hotel to the temple. Which I figured was pretty good going. I growled into the parking lot and saw her Ferrari was still there. So I climbed out of the Lamborghini and stood staring at the temple like I hadn't seen her car.

The Stupa is a striking building. It's said to be the largest in Europe. It looks like a vast, white candlestick, a hundred and eight feet tall, with a glistening, gold dome and spire, perched on the edge of a cliff towering over the glistening Mediterranean below. I shoved my hands in my pocket and climbed the steps to the broad platform where the Stupa sits. There was a small crowd of tourists, taking photographs, and another small group was emerging from the magnificent wooden doors at the top of the flight of sixteen steps.

There was no sign of Rafaela, so I climbed those sixteen steps and passed through the huge doorway into the meditation room. It was shaded and quiet, and directly opposite the door was a vast golden statue of the Buddha. He didn't look like he was worried about much, and for a moment I envied him. I looked around, but the place was empty. Sounds echoed from outside, but they somehow didn't seem to penetrate the stillness of the room. I noticed a flight of steps over on the left that led down to some kind of museum. They were cordoned off and there was a tall, lanky guy with very short hair standing there watching me. After a moment he said, "Welcome," in an accent I couldn't place.

"Thanks, I'm looking..."

He chuckled and didn't give me time to finish. "We are all looking. Like a cat chasing its tail."

I smiled and blinked and nodded. "I guess that's true. In this particular case I am looking for something concrete."

"Like a vall." He meant wall, but he said vall.

"Like a woman."

His eyes went wide. "Oooh," he said.

"She owns the Ferrari outside."

His mouth spread as wide as his eyes. "Aaaah! Very nice."

"I wonder if you've seen her. She's very beautiful, very Spanish..."

"Spanish women are very beautiful." I nodded and waited and he grinned at me. After a moment he pointed at the big, bright door behind me. "Maybe she is also looking for you."

I turned and she was standing silhouetted black against the glare. She was staring at the statue and didn't seem to be aware of me. I turned back to the tall, lanky guy. "Thanks."

He was still grinning. "Angry Buddha," he said suddenly. "There is also angry Buddha."

I nodded, repeated, "Thanks," and crossed the meditation room to where Rafaela was standing in a low-cut crimson dress. When I was standing beside her she turned and flicked her eyes over my face.

"How did you know I was here?"

"I didn't."

She turned her eyes back to the Buddha. "He looks so peaceful, doesn't he?"

"He's detached, that's why. We are attached."

She didn't answer for a moment, then said, "You and I?"

"Maybe."

"Is that how you found me here?"

"Sure. It could be."

"Things are not always what they seem, are they?" I thought she was going to step out into the winter sunlight, but instead she moved in among the shadows and went to stand at the foot of the statue, looking up into that peaceful face, with tears in her eyes. "Do you think perhaps I should meditate? Do you think I should try to find a spiritual path?"

TEN

They were questions I wouldn't have bothered to answer when I was eighteen and trying to pick girls up in bars. I sure as hell wasn't going to start now. So I said nothing and she turned and stared into my face for a moment, then made her way back to the door. I followed her down the steps, while she continued with her philosophical window-shopping.

"Do you think, if I followed some kind of spiritual path, it might give my life meaning?" She crossed the broad paved terrace and leaned on the iron railing, looking down at the ocean. She didn't seem to expect an answer, because she kept on talking. "Everything seems so meaningless sometimes. So pointless. Is that existentialism? What path do you think I should follow? Should I become a Buddhist? Or perhaps return to Catholicism, and become a nun? Maybe I could do Zen, or study Tao."

I was getting bored so I cut in. "I don't know, Rafaela. Hasn't Armani designed a spiritual path you could buy at the Emporio in New York?"

"That was unkind."

"Yeah?" Something in my voice made her turn and look at me. I went on. "You were talking shit. A spiritual path, if there is such a thing, is not a designer label that you can put on or take off depending on what mood you are in that day. And it does not give your life meaning. It's a commitment to finding the truth—about yourself. Are you sure that's something you want to do?"

She arched an exquisite eyebrow. "I didn't know you were a guru. Perhaps I should come to you to find my spiritual path."

"I wouldn't recommend it."

"Where did you disappear to this morning?"

"I had some business I needed to attend to."

"What kind of business?"

I smiled. "None of *your* business."

"Now you've slept with me you think you can treat me like trash?"

"Maybe that's part of your spiritual path."

"Why have you followed me here, Harry?"

"Stop flattering yourself, Rafaela. You're cute, but you're not that cute. I heard the Stupa and the Butterfly House in Benalmádena were two must sees. So I came to see."

"I heard you asking the man upstairs..."

"Come on, Rafaela! How many Ferraris do you see parked down there in the lot? I arrived, saw the Ferrari and went to look for you. Stop before you embarrass yourself."

She snorted. "You know how to make a girl feel special."

"You want to grab some lunch?"

"Sure, why not?" She was mad at me and I was wondering why she didn't just walk away. "We can go into the *Pueblo. Fidel's* is nice."

We made our way toward the parking lot. There I spotted a Range Rover parked near the exit, and a guy with short hair and a moustache sitting with his ass on the trunk of her Ferrari. I made like I hadn't seen him and said, "Wait for me by the car, will you? I have to go to the john."

I watched her trot down the steps to the lot and pulled back toward the temple wall. Through the crowd I saw another guy join the moustache. He had a ponytail and was dressed in the same kind of non-uniform, only his leather jacket was brown instead of black. Rafaela didn't flinch in her step. The car lights flashed and bleeped and the moustache pushed off the car and stepped toward her. He said something I couldn't hear. She reached for the car door like he wasn't there. He grabbed her wrist and she tried to wrench free. His friend moved in and grabbed her arm. People stopped to stare. She was struggling and they were dragging her toward the sidewalk and the Range Rover. I sprinted.

I took the steps to the parking lot in a single leap and in four strides I'd crossed the lot to the Ferrari and vaulted the hood. The ponytail came at me, snarling and ugly, pointing. "Stay out of this!"

"Let her go! Don't make me hurt you!"

Behind him I could see the moustache dragging her, kicking and screaming toward the Range Rover. Ponytail yelled, "*Get outta here!*" and rushed me, swinging a right hook at my head that would have broken my jaw if it had connected. It didn't connect because I hunkered down and let it sail over my head. Then I pushed up with my legs and drove an uppercut into his solar plexus. He made an ugly retching noise that sounded oddly astonished and dropped to the sidewalk. He wasn't getting up.

I sprinted again. Two strides got me to where the moustache was trying to cram Rafaela into the back of the truck. I shouted and he spun to meet me. His style was tae kwon do. When practiced by a real expert, it can be devastating. It is fast and powerful, but you have to be the right size. If you are too big, you're too slow.

I saw his feet coming two or three seconds before they arrived: a side kick to the head followed by a spinning back kick and a flying scissor kick. It was spectacular, but gave me time to draft my will and contemplate various options for retirement while he finished his version of *Swan Lake*.

I leaned away from the side kick, ducked the roundhouse and when he went into his scissor kick I was on his right side instead of in front of him and drove my right fist into his floating ribs as he came down.

He went down on his knees and I stepped past him to take Rafaela in my arms and guide her toward the Lamborghini.

"Come on, let me get you out of here."

She was staring wide-eyed past my shoulder as the two guys staggered back to the Range Rover. I bundled her into the passenger seat and got behind the wheel. Moustache and Ponytail were still vomiting in the gutter as we made the circle and passed the Butterfly House, headed for the freeway.

"What the hell was that?" she asked, staring into my face.

I snorted something that might have been a laugh. "You tell me. Your husband's the billionaire! Put your seat belt on."

She took some time to react, then snapped her belt closed. "Who were those men?"

"You're asking me?" I shook my head. "Ask your husband. I don't know how he allows you to go around the way you do. I don't know how you've survived this long. I figured you just had bodyguards lingering in the background. You don't even have that."

We came to *Higueron* and I passed under the overpass and joined the freeway headed back toward Marbella.

"Call your husband. Tell him what happened. Tell him I'm taking you home and you need someone to go get your car from the Stupa. And for Christ's sake tell him to get you a bodyguard. People like you don't have the luxury of wandering around the streets as and when you please."

She sat through all this in silence, her eyes wide, shifting this way and then that, like she was trying to make sense of what happened. I scowled and snapped, "Rafaela!"

"What...?"

"Your phone. Call your husband. He needs to know what happened."

She nodded and reached for her cell.

She held it to her ear and after a moment spoke quietly, *"Papi, soy Rafi..."*

She was quiet for a bit, then rattled away in Andalusian Spanish that I couldn't follow. She was quiet some more, then said, *"OK, vale. Voy para casa."* She was on her way home.

When she'd hung up I said, "Papi?"

"Don't start getting paranoid. It's a nickname because he is older than me. I call him Papi."

"What did you tell him?"

"That something has happened. I need to tell him about it. And that you had helped me. I told him I am going home."

I came off onto the toll road but took it easy, giving her time to talk. After a moment she said, "He wasn't happy you helped me."

"He'd have preferred you were abducted?"

"No."

She didn't say anymore so I glanced at her, asking her to explain. She sighed.

"He is very jealous. He is possessive, territorial. He did not want me abducted, but he does not want me being with other men. A man protecting me, saving me from kidnapping..." She shrugged. "That is a threat to him."

"Jesus..." We drove in silence a bit longer. Then I asked her, "Is it worth it? The Ferrari, the pool, the mansion, first-class travel, all the five-star hotels—is it worth the price?"

"I don't know. Maybe. Perhaps freedom is overrated; if it exists at all."

I came off where she told me, at La Cañada, and followed the A-355 inland, past the cemetery of the Virgin of the Vineyard of God. We reached *Calle Montua* and began to climb toward her house. She didn't speak until we had pulled up outside her gate. Then she leaned forward and kissed me.

"Thank you for last night. Thank you for wanting to help me."

She opened the door and I stopped her. "So, what now?"

"Go!"

She got out and ran to the gate. I turned the Hurracán around and made my way back down the hill. In my mirror I saw the gate open and I saw her slip inside. As the gate closed, so I shut her out of my mind.

I had asked the brigadier if an electromagnetic pulse would neutralize the detonators on the bombs, but I knew the answer already. They would. Unless the detonator was mechanical, something like a tripwire or a hammer, it had to be electronic. If it was electronic, an EMP with a field of ten to twelve feet could knock out both bombs. Such an EMP device could be delivered to the site under cover of darkness by a drone with night-vision cameras.

So why hadn't the Spanish authorities already thought of that?

That was not hard to imagine. For a start the kids' father would want to vet any operation to rescue the kids, and if he was any kind of a father his instinct would be to veto anything and everything that might put his kids at risk. And that could well include the fear that an electromagnetic pulse might trigger the bombs instead of neutralizing them.

Plus, he had probably not even notified Madrid of what had happened, for fear they might take control of the operation out of his hands.

So stage one of any rescue plan, I told myself as I wound down out of the hills, would be to deliver an EMP device via drone and place it beneath the rear axle of the bus. Part two would be more difficult. I had not analyzed the photographs and footage yet, but I figured there had to be at least a dozen guards at the place. At night there might be four to six on duty. The area was small and they would probably all be in sight of each other. So the idea would be to knock them out, one way or another, hook the bus up to one of those tractors and pull it back from the ravine, and then remove the mines.

Another option was to remove the mines first. I could do that by climbing up from the ravine, then let the *Guardia Civil* pull the bus back from the edge once they saw the mines were gone. But I didn't like that option because each mine was going to weigh in the region of ten to twelve pounds. Removing twenty to twenty-four pounds from the rear of the bus could make it over-balance and plunge into the ravine.

Probably the simplest option would be to set off the EMP and get the brigadier to inform the Spanish authorities that the detonators had been deactivated. But I didn't like that option either. Because it meant pulling out before the danger had been fully neutralized, and leaving the job in the hands of people I did not fully trust.

On the other hand, rendering six cops senseless, without anyone noticing and without starting a firefight, was not going to be easy.

The third option, and one which had definite merit, was to go get hold of Baldomero and start feeding him piecemeal to hungry rats until he had the mines deactivated. But attractive as that option was, it was probably also the most difficult of them all, and would require time: precious time I did not have.

And then there was the official option. Back off, let Baldomero and General José Ferrer García reach an accommodation, and then go in for the kill. The problem with that option was that, the more I thought about it, the more convinced I became that Baldomero Omeya was not going to let the kids go. You could bet your bottom dollar there was not a shred of evidence to connect Omeya to that bus, but each one of those kids, the teachers and the adults, were all potential witnesses who could give evidence that might just lead to someone who might identify someone who might identify Omeya. They were links in a potential chain of evidence, and my gut told me Omeya was a man who hedged his bets. Hedging his bets in this case meant, once the cargo was safely out of Spain, blowing the mines and killing the kids, the parents and the teachers. Destroying the potential chain of evidence.

I didn't mean to let that happen, but I didn't know how to stop it.

As I climbed out of the Lamborghini and threw the keys to the kid from valet parking, I could feel the hot coals of rage beginning to smolder in my gut. I needed an EMP, I needed equipment, I needed a tranquilizer gun. I needed to get to that damned bus and I needed the brigadier to step up and make it happen. But he was playing coy. He knew as well as I did that if those kids were not extracted from that bus they were going to die. So why the "don't do anything to put them at risk" bullshit? I'd say dangling over a precipice, sitting on two mines and a gas tank full of fuel, they were already at risk.

I had called him too many times, and I knew if I called again it would probably be counterproductive. So instead of going to my room to stew, I went to the bar and ordered a large Macallan, which I took to a corner table to sip while I turned the thing over. The first sip I took fueled the coals in my belly into a hot burn.

As things stood I could not rely on the brigadier or on Cobra. The mission had been aborted and I had been ordered to stand down. So I had only one person I could rely on and that was me. Therefore I needed somehow to acquire or make an EMP device light enough to attach to the drone, and powerful enough to eradiate an area of ten to fifteen feet. I needed also an arms supplier who could get me a crossbow and a supply of darts with a narcotic agent powerful enough to knock out at least half a dozen cops. And I needed all that by tomorrow night.

And I just couldn't see how I could do that.

That was when my cell phone rang. I looked at the screen and saw, Rafaela.

ELEVEN

"You're hard to get rid of."

"My husband wants to meet you."

"No kidding."

"He was furious."

"I should have let you be abducted?"

She was quiet for a moment, like she didn't understand what I'd said. Irony obviously wasn't the big thing with her. Finally she said, "No, he has always told me I should stay at home, or take one of his men as a bodyguard. But I have always insisted on my independence. Now he is using this to punish me."

"So why does he want to meet me?"

"He suspects we are lovers. I told him that was ridiculous."

I was thinking fast. "So what's to stop him having his boys stick me headfirst in the pool for half an hour?"

"Harry!" She sounded genuinely horrified. "We are not animals!"

"My mistake. What's to stop him paying somebody else to do it for him?"

"Stop it, please. This is not America! He has asked me to invite you to a party. He wants to meet you in person and see for himself that you are nothing to me."

"Nice."

"What we feel must be our secret."

"Sure. I think I can manage that. When is this party?"

"Tonight."

"*Tonight?*"

"It is a small reunion of friends on his yacht in Puerto Banus. It has been planned for a couple of weeks. My husband entertains very much."

"It's short notice."

"You have somewhere else you need to be? Maybe I can come to you after the party. Please, Harry."

"No, sure. I'll be there. Where, what time?"

"I will come and collect you. We will go together."

"That should put your husband's mind at rest."

"I will see you at eight."

I hung up and spent thirty seconds walking around my suite swearing violently and imaginatively. Finally I grabbed my phone and called the brigadier again.

"Harry, this has to stop."

"Listen to me. He has invited me to a party tonight on his yacht in Puerto Banus."

"That could seriously endanger those children."

"That's bullshit and you know it. Those kids were as good as dead from the moment the bus was snatched. The only chance of survival they have is if somebody removes those bombs."

"And how do you propose to do that from a party in Puerto Banus?"

"I don't. Stay with me and hear me out. His wife—"

"His *wife?*"

"Maybe it's his daughter. That's not important. She's collecting me at eight this evening to go to the party."

"Harry, *why* has he invited you to a party onboard his yacht?"

"Because he wants to meet me. Listen, will you, sir?"

"Harry, *why* does Omeya want to meet you?"

I sighed noisily. "Because I helped his wife-daughter out of a tight spot earlier today. I told you..."

"The two Company agents you beat up earlier today? It's too soon. I understood you were setting up a play for after the *Princess Diana* had departed."

"This is the way it has played out, sir." He grunted. I went on, "The point is, he must have a study or an office on the yacht. If I can get in maybe I can find something to connect Omeya with the bus and the hijack..."

"You're dreaming, Harry."

"Or—just hear me out, sir! Or, something to connect him with the *Princess Diana*."

"The what?"

"I told you, I took a drive to Cadiz, the *Princess Diana* is the container ship that entered port yesterday from the States. It was the only one flying an American flag. I asked around and they told me she was due to be unloaded in the next day or so. I have no proof that it's the boat, but the timing fits. Not just with the hijacking of the container, but with the hijacking of the bus here. If he is applying pressure to General José Ferrer García with this kidnapping, his timing would have to be pretty precise."

It was his turn to sigh. "If it was shipped to Spain—and I grant you it probably was—it could be in Cadiz, Algeciras, Malaga... Harry, it could be in Barcelona or Morocco."

"Yes, or it could be in Cadiz. And the *Princess Diana is* in Cadiz, and probably departed the US a week ago. If—*if*—I find just one piece of paper in his office that makes reference to the *Princess Diana*, we can be ninety percent certain that the cargo stolen from Groom Lake is on that ship."

"Fair enough, but what about the children? The risk to them is unthinkable."

"You're wrong, sir. They are only at risk at that stage if he connects me with US law enforcement, if he thinks I am CIA or DIA. But as far as I know neither the CIA nor the DIA drive around in Lamborghinis or stay at five-star hotels."

"A Lamborghini?"

"I believe it was you who told me once, sir, 'If you want to go unnoticed among tigers, you have to wear stripes.'"

"How very colorful of me. So you are playing the playboy."

"An opportunist, seducing his beautiful young wife, snooping in his office, but just an opportunist. And that's *if* I get caught. Which I won't. Now, part two—"

"Part two?"

"Yes, sir, part two. In case I do not find some way of disabling the detonators in his office, I need, urgently, by tonight, an EMP light enough to mount on a drone but powerful enough to blow out an area of ten to fifteen feet. And I need a crossbow with two dozen tranquilizer darts powerful enough to knock out four to six big men."

"Out of the question."

"Sir, you know it's the only way."

"It is out of the question, Harry! They'll shut us down! We *cannot* put the children's lives at risk!"

"Sir! If we do not remove those bombs, those children are already dead!"

He waited a heartbeat, then: "I'm sorry, Harry, I can't authorize it."

I hung up and spent the next fifteen minutes trying to work out where in Malaga I could get hold of a ten-thousand-volt portable power supply that was light enough to be carried by my drone. It wasn't a productive session because I kept circling back to the fact that the brigadier had the contacts in military research and development to access that kind of device. But the most powerful EMP device I could put together in the next few hours would have an effective range of maybe three inches.

If I went with that it would mean making two, carrying the damned things to the site and holding them within an inch of each mine and discharging them simultaneously. Aside from the virtual impossibility of the plan, there was the risk that if one mine was disabled first, it might trigger the other. I was trapped in a double bind, and I hadn't even started to think about where to get tranquilizer darts.

If I'd been in Mexico, Medellín or Bangkok it would have been a different story. There I had friends and contacts. But the SAS did not make a habit of mounting operations on the Costa del Sol. I had no contacts here—except the brigadier. And so it went, round and round.

By six PM I had made four phone calls and achieved exactly nothing. I was offered semiautomatics, automatics, bazookas and rocket launchers. But requests for EMPs and tranquilizer darts elicited nothing but laughter.

At seven I resigned myself to the fact that the plan was not viable and I would have to either find Omeya's remote detonator, or abduct Omeya and threaten to castrate him with an improvised flint knife to make him give the order for the detonators to be disabled. I had no plan for that, and Rafaela was going to collect me at eight, so I showered and shaved and pulled on a suitably expensive evening suit of the sort the brigadier and Ian Fleming would have approved.

THE PARTY WAS everything you'd expect from a billionaire yacht-party at Puerto Banus. Ninety percent of the fifty guests (it was just a small gathering) were mere millionaires working the bellows to keep Omeya's ego suitably inflated. The other ten percent consisted of two European commissioners, one Hollywood star, a Spanish cabinet minister and a Mexican drug baron.

Rafaela, who'd collected me in a chauffeur-driven Bentley, had slipped into a deep purple satin dress with a slash all the way down one of her shapely, brown legs to the strap of her purple satin high heels. It was the kind of dress, and the kind of slash, that got your testosterone all confused, beating its chest and gnashing its teeth.

We boarded the yacht via the aft deck platform and stepped into a crowded saloon, with Rafaela's arm linked through mine. A waiter in a white jacket approached us, bowed and offered us a tray with chilled glasses of champagne. People recognized Rafaela and approached to greet her, and eyed me with curiosity, wondering if I would soon be appearing in the Marbella gossip columns.

I leaned in to her. "Your husband is not going to like you drifting around hanging on my arm like this."

"But I am enjoying it. He is on the upper deck anyway, by the pool. He practically lives there. We will go up and I will introduce you now."

There was an elevator, because real yachts have elevators, and we rode it to the upper deck and stepped out into a throng of white tuxedos and glittering dresses, each one with a grinning person inside it. The ratio of Botox to flesh was about sixty-forty among the men and sixty-twenty among the women, where the other twenty percent was cohesive silicon gel.

We maneuvered our way through the rigid breasts and rigid, grinning faces toward a huge man in an open-neck shirt and a tweed jacket, who was standing, holding court beside the pool. He had a large head with very short, white hair, an eagle nose and dark, olive skin. He had a big, barrel chest and a massive presence. He saw us approaching and he opened his arms to Rafaela.

"*Cariño mío!*" he boomed. "*Ven y dame un* kiss!"

She giggled, they hugged and he gave her a peck on the lips. Now his eyes found me for the first time and though he was smiling and welcoming in his manner, his eyes wanted to gut me and feed me to his dogs.

"And, so, you are Mr. Harry Reid." He spread his hands and laughed. "Not my good friend the leader of the Senate, because he is already dead."

I laughed. "Already?"

"We must all, my friend, as chimney sweepers, come to dust!"

"I guess we must. No, I am not that Harry Reid."

"When my *Cari* told me she had been rescued from abductors

by Harry Reid, I thought, he is like Obi Wan Kenobi, more terrible when dead than alive!"

I shook my head. "No, no. I am more terrible alive than dead."

"Be careful, Mr. Reid," he wagged a large finger at me, "at the moment we prefer you alive. Ensure it stays that way."

"I'll do my best."

He looked at me from under his eyebrows and I noticed the whites of his eyes were yellow. "But seriously," he said and stepped close to me, taking my elbow and guiding me away from the group, toward the gunwale. "I must thank you for what you did. It was very courageous, and my gratitude knows no limits. Rafaela, my *Cari*, is everything to me. I do not know what I would do without her, or if I lost her."

I watched his face as he spoke, then gave my head a small shake. "No thanks are necessary, Mr. Omeya. I am sure anyone would have done the same."

There was something sly about his smile when he said, "But from what she tells me, few would have had the skill."

"Oh, well, I stay in shape."

"Tell me, please, exactly what happened. How did you happen to meet at the Stupa?"

"It was pure luck. I am here on holiday, I asked the concierge what there was to see and do around here and he told me I should visit the Butterfly House and the Buddhist temple. I went and happened to bump into Rafaela."

"You had of course already met at Puerto Banus, when you literally bumped into each other."

"One of the many evils of cell phones. Nobody looks where they are going anymore."

"Remarkable. And she was on her way to her car, and you were on your way to the lavatories, when these two men attacked her."

There was a kind of madness in his eyes, like he was about to break into crazy laughter. I watched him a second and nodded.

"Yeah, I had suggested we grab a bit of lunch, but I needed to go to the john. I happened to look back, and I saw this guy grabbing her wrist."

"And you flew into action, like a Marvel hero." The sarcasm was palpable. I wondered whether to ignore it or confront it. He moved on before I could decide. "What do you do, Mr. Reid?"

I laughed. "For a living? Not a lot. I have some investments. They give me enough to live on."

"Enough to rent a Lamborghini."

The emphasis was on *rent*. I nodded. "Enough to do that, yes."

"You will forgive me if I have misjudged you, Mr. Reid. But how much do you need to just go away?"

The question was delivered in an amiable, chatty style and surprised me. I let my face show it and followed up with a scowl. "I don't need anything, Mr. Omeya. If I am unwelcome I'll leave. You invited me here, remember?"

His eyes had become poisonous. "Yes, I remember. Because I wanted to get a look at the young man who had engineered two accidental meetings with my wife. And now that I have looked at you, Mr. Reid, I have decided that I do not like you. You have the stink of a military man and the eyes of a predator. So I ask you again, what do I have to give you to make you go away?"

I didn't answer straight away. I took my time to study his face and his venomous, yellow eyes. Then I put my finger on his chest and spoke quietly.

"I'll tell you what I need from you, Mr. Omeya. Exactly nothing. I have the stink of a military man? Yeah, because I was eight years in British special forces. And the eyes of a predator, maybe. Like you, like any man who has learned that in this life you have to fight to get what you want. Did I engineer a meeting with your wife? Yeah, I did, the first time. I saw her and she was the woman with the most class on Puerto Banus. So I bumped into her to make her acquaintance. And when she told me she was married I stepped away. I was at the Stupa to see the Stupa, not to see your wife. Because what I have is mine. It's not stolen. I don't need to steal another man's woman or another man's money. So you can shove your payoff wherever it fits and I'll be on my way."

He closed his eyes and raised both hands like I was pointing a gun at him.

"Please, wait. You must forgive me, Mr. Reid. A man my age, with my fortune and a wife as beautiful as mine, cannot afford to be off his guard. Everywhere there are predators and parasites, seeking to steal from a man like me."

"Yeah, well I am not one of them. I don't want your money or your wife. If you'll forgive me, I think I should go."

"Please, accept my apology, Harry. You have saved my *Cari's* life and I have been unspeakably rude. Stay, allow me to make you a gift." He raised both hands again. "Not money! I will not insult you by offering you money. But please accept Karina." He glanced around, spotted a blonde by the pool and waved to her to come. "Karina is exquisite. She is yours as long as you are in Marbella. My treat. Enjoy yourself at the party, and anything you need, I am eternally in your debt."

He patted me on the arm and moved away like a vast Spanish galleon easing out of harbor. A moment later Karina was standing in front of me, smiling with perfect teeth.

"Hi," she said.

I was still trying to make sense of what had just happened. I blinked at her a couple of times and nodded. "Hi."

"You're one of Baldomero's special friends?"

"I guess I must be," I said. "What do you think?"

She grinned and winked. "I think you must be too."

TWELVE

WE HAD A DRINK AND DISCUSSED THE RELATIVE VALUES of rain and sunshine, and compared the beaches of the Caribbean with those of the Med, and agreed that those in the eastern Med were almost as good as those in the Caribbean. Having exhausted those topics I asked her, "Do you mind if I take you somewhere private and tie you up?"

Her face lit up. "That would be *fun!* Let me just go get some coke!"

She toddled off at an awkward run. When she returned five minutes later she wasn't carrying a red and white can in her hand. She had a small wooden box instead, and a bottle of rum by the neck. She winked at me and giggled. "Rum and coke."

"You're cute."

"I know."

"You know the boat?"

She whispered in my ear about the things she'd done in just about every cabin on the yacht. I was impressed and whispered back, "You know where Omeya's office is?"

She started to say, "All his work he does on deck by the pool..."

I interrupted her with a wink. "But he must have an office, you know, that we can borrow…"

She gasped. "You're bad!"

"And dangerous. You know where it is?"

"Of course. We can go!"

"Who has the key?"

"Baldo and his secretary. But we don't need key."

"We don't?"

She giggled again and shook her head. "His secretary is in the office. Baldo was yelling at her to get some job finished. Some shipping from New York."

"That's exciting. She?"

"Anja. She's *gorgeous!* But she's kind of German."

I winked. "Let's go talk to her. Sounds like she could use a rum and coke."

"*Seriously?*" Her eyes were wide with wonder.

"Seriously."

I followed her through a saloon, down some carpeted stairs and along a corridor with highly polished mahogany panels on the walls. Eventually we came to a door with a shiny brass handle. She knocked, grinned at me and bobbed with excitement. A voice straight out of Nietzsche's wet dreams yelled, "*Ja?*"

Karina grinned at me and I nodded encouragement. She called, "It's Karina. I have something for you. Can I come in?"

The reply came with an edge of irritability. It sounded like, "Yacom!"

Karina opened the door and went in. I slipped in after her, pulling my P226 from the pancake at the small of my back.

Anja was beautiful the way a large iceberg is beautiful. You look at it, think, "Wow!" and then shiver. She probably glimmered in the sunshine. She had platinum hair, blue eyes and skin the color of Alpine milk. She frowned at Karina and then scowled at me as I closed the door.

"Who are you?"

"I am a very dear friend of Baldo's." I said it as I strode around the desk, put the Sig Sauer to her head and dragged her to her feet. I pulled her to the middle of the room and then snarled, "Get on your knees."

Karina was gaping at me. I gave her a secret grin and said, "Put the coke and the rum on the desk. Let's have a party."

She did as I said and I glanced around the room. It's surprising how few things there are you can use to tie somebody up in an office since wireless technology hit the scene. I said to Karina, "OK, listen carefully, I want you to take off Anja's blouse and her bra. Understood?"

Anja spluttered, "You are insane! You know what vill happen to you?"

"Speak only when spoken to, Anja. And everything will be fine."

Karina had got Anja's blouse off and had taken some time out to have a quick snort from her little box. I was about to tell her to get a move on when she offered some to Anja, who took a snort too. Then they both started giggling and Karina offered some to me. I shook my head. "Later. The bra."

"Oh! Yes, the bra!"

They both started laughing and Anja helped Karina remove her bra and hand it to me. I used it to tie Anja's hands behind her back while Karina told her, "This is wild."

"Ja, but I heff so much vork!"

I pulled her to her feet and snarled, "Lie facedown on the couch."

Karina grabbed her arm, still giggling. "Come on! Just take a break! It'll be fun. I'll help you."

As she lay down I told Karina, "Use her blouse to tie her ankles. Tie them tight!"

When she'd done that I told her, "Now take off your clothes and lie next to her."

After more giggling and another snort each she did that. I used her bra to tie her wrists and her dress to tie her ankles. How I gagged them I will leave to the reader's imagination.

After that I sat at the desk. The computer was switched on and running because Anja had been working. I didn't waste time trying to read anything. I searched the drawers and found a pen drive, then dumped everything I could see into it in a kind of wild cyber sacking. And while the stuff was transferring, I ransacked the office. I found nothing relating to the *Princess Diana*, and there was no sign of a remote detonator, or any suggestion of who might have it.

The giggles from the sofa had slowly turned into whimpers, with the occasional muffled squeak of rage from Anja. I went over and hunkered down beside their heads, placed the barrel of the Sig a few inches from Anja's nose and spoke quietly but deliberately.

"Baldo is expecting a shipment from New York, right?"

Anja nodded. Her eyes did not waver from the barrel of the P226.

"That shipment has arrived aboard the *Princess Diana*, correct?"

Now her eyes flicked to mine and she nodded again. I had just confirmed something I no longer doubted, but it was something. Now I asked, "Who takes care of security for Omeya?"

She went very still and swallowed. I frowned. "If somebody needs discipline, maybe punishment. Who organizes it?" She swallowed harder. I arched my eyebrows high and smiled. "*You?*"

She gave a small nod. She was terrified and she was no hero. I reached across Karina's head and eased down the gag on Anja's mouth.

"You take care of business?"

"Why not? Baldo tells me what he wants. I convey it to the men."

"OK, so I am going to ask you a very simple question. And if you lie, or give me any trouble, this is going to get very ugly. You understand?"

She gave a tiny nod and Karina started to cry.

"Where is the detonator."

Anja went very pale. "What detonator?"

"The bus, in Cazorla. I need the detonator for the bombs, and I need it now."

Her voice was barely a whisper. "There is no detonator…"

"You have to be kidding me."

"Please don't kill me."

"But, if they attempt…" I paused.

She said, "What…?"

I frowned. "If they…"

"If they what?"

"Jesus!"

Suddenly the whole thing was crystal clear. I had been staring at it, I had skirted around it, but I had not seen it clearly till that moment. My belly burned with rage and fear. I got to my feet and as I stood there was a rap on the door. I turned and glared at Anja. She held my eye for a second and let out a scream that would have frozen the blood of the gods. Next thing she was screaming, thrashing and squirming like a demented Aryan worm. Her wild movements knocked Karina sprawling on the floor and the door burst open.

There were two of them. They both had crew cuts, they were both big and they both had mercenary written all over them. The one holding the door was shorter and broader across the shoulders, with a thick bull neck and piggy eyes. The man behind him was a bit younger, taller, gaunt with very pale blue eyes. When he spoke he had a flat, ugly South African accent.

"What the fuck…?"

The guy with his hand on the door said, "Son of a bitch…" He was American.

I slammed my left heel into the floor and lunged, smashing my right foot into the door. It was a heavy, mahogany affair and hammered hard into the bull neck's nose. He backed away into his pal, with his hand over his nose and blood spilling through his fingers. I didn't wait to see what happened next. I lunged again and drove a right hook into his floating ribs and kicked him hard in the belly. They both collapsed backward in a heap and I ran out the door.

I had made the stairs when I heard the first shouts coming after me. Aside from, *"Get the bastard!"* and *"Stop the mother-fucker!"* they also kept shouting *"Over!"* which gave me a clue they were talking on the radio. Which meant I was probably running into the arms of a mercenary army. And as I bounded up the stairs a bunch of startled beautiful people screamed and backed away as four gorillas in Italian evening suits converged at the top of the steps.

The first gorilla, who had all his hair on his upper lip, bounded down the stairs at me. His second bound landed his crotch on my right uppercut. He made a very feminine noise and started to weep as I shoved him in the way of his three pals, who stumbled and staggered over him, trying not to fall down the stairs.

It was a couple of precious seconds I needed to make the pool deck. As I did so I pulled the Sig from my pancake and fired a shot into the ceiling. Everybody either cowered or hit the floor and I sprinted, dodging and leaping over beautiful, expensive people who were all screaming at the same time.

Behind me I heard feet on the stairs and I burst out onto the deck, where everybody was hiding behind furniture, except Baldomero Omeya, who stood huge and apparently fearless, framed by the luminous, turquoise glow of his swimming pool. I strode toward him with the Sig held out in front of me in both hands, trained on his enormous head.

"You're coming with me, pal!"

He shook his huge head. "No."

"If I have to cut you into small pieces," I snarled, "you are coming with me!"

His face was pure contempt. He jerked his head behind me. "Pah! Touch me and they will kill you."

I turned to look. There was bull neck, his blue-eyed South African pal and the three gorillas, all pointing weapons at me.

It was a fraction of a second. The thought flashed into my mind to move behind Omeya, and in that instant the Blue Eyes' weapon flashed. The pain seared into my hand and burned up my arm as the slug hit my Sig and tore it out of my hand.

I staggered back. Omeya bellowed something about not killing his guests, and before I could react I saw the South African charging at me with a blade in his hand. My arm was useless, so I ran at him and kicked him in the knee. He slashed at my leg and missed, and I kicked hum hard in the knee again. Whole seconds were passing by and I knew I was in serious trouble. Blue Eyes' pals were surrounding me, my arm was in agony and I was three stories above the port.

He lunged at me again. He was tough but I could tell his leg was hurting. So I feinted a kick at his knee and as he faltered I smashed my elbow into his chin. As he went down I snatched his Glock from under his arm and shot one of the gorillas between the eyes. I was aiming for his heart, but my arm was not responding.

The other four backed up and I trained the gun on Omeya. A phone rang. A man lying on the floor said, "It's the cops..."

Omeya snarled, "Tell them everything is fine, just a bit of fun."

I told him, "I'll be back for you. If you're lucky, I'll kill you. But if anything happens to those kids, I swear you'll be begging me to kill you."

He spat elaborately. "Words. You'll be dead before dawn."

I vaulted the gunwale and plunged into the water. It was cold, turned icy by the winter North Atlantic feeding in through the Straits of Gibraltar, and the icy chill brought the blood beating back into my arms. I went deep and swum toward the dock. Pretty soon I came to some smaller yachts, eased between them and pulled myself out. When I'd made it onto the quay, spilling water onto the narrow decks as I went, I looked back toward the sparkling yacht, flashing lights and thudding music like a floating nightclub. In odd contrast to its appearance, the upper deck was lined with almost motionless people staring down into the water. Among them I could make out Omeya's massive silhouette.

I stood a moment, in the shadow of the smaller boats, wringing the water from my clothes and watching. I became aware of a steady flow of men spilling from the yacht and fanning out, not very discretely, searching among the cars and the crowds. I had no problem meeting them—in fact right then I would have welcomed it—but I was in a hurry. After what Anja had told me I was in a serious hurry, and I had no time to waste venting my rage.

I ducked down into the *Calle Benabola*, and sprinted to the end where it joined the José Banús Circus. I needed a weapon, I needed less conspicuous, dry clothes, and above all I needed a vehicle. Something told me I was not going to have to wait very long.

I crossed the road to Julio Iglesias Avenue (seriously) and stood in the shadow of the pine trees that lined the pedestrian walkway. Pretty soon a dark blue Audi pulled up with two of the gorillas sitting in the front. I stepped out of the shadows and stood in the road in front of them. Two things I was certain of. Omeya really wanted to get me alone in a room strapped to a chair, and, that being the case, these two proto-simians were not going to kill me. What they were going to do was get out of the car and try to wrestle me into their back seat.

Sure enough, they pulled into the side of the road and put their hazards on, and as the cars behind them began to stream slowly past, they climbed out and came for me, one on either side. I moved to the right of the hood, where the traffic was, so I had the driver facing me and his pal on the other side of the car. The driver came at me with an ugly look on his face, and I remembered Bruce Lee's timeless words on the essence of fighting. He said, "You gotta *honestly express yourself!*"

And that was what I did. I made a short pendulum skip and smashed my right heel into his knee. Then, so fast it was virtually simultaneous, I smashed a straight right into his nose, opened up into a straight left into his solar plexus, backhanded my right fist into his temple, drove a left hook into his liver and tore his head off with a right hook to his jaw. If he wasn't dead when he hit the ground he should have been.

Meantime his pal was halfway across the hood of the Audi. A right front kick with my instep sent his balls on a one-way hike to his brain, where they belonged. Honestly express yourself. It's what it was all about.

I climbed into the Audi and took off back toward the Puente Romano. On the way I pulled my cell from my soaking pocket and called the brigadier. I didn't let him start. I snarled at him, "Now you listen to me and you listen good. There is no remote detonator. You got that? Do you understand that? Do you understand what that means? It means there is no failsafe and there is no way to kill the motion sensors. It means that if the *Guardia Civil* try to pull the bus from the ravine, nobody is going to detonate the bombs remotely, not even if the motion sensors fail! *Do you understand that?*" I was half yelling down the phone. "*Do you understand what that means?*"

There was silence at the other end. I shouted, "*It means there is no way to defuse the mines, because they have no intention of letting those kids go! They never did! It means those damned mines are on an automatic timer set to detonate after the damned ship leaves port!*" The silence in the car as I sped along the coast toward Marbella was deafening. I shouted again, trying to block out the awful silence, "*It means that all the time we were trying not to put those kids at risk, they were getting closer to death!*"

Still nothing. I roared, "*Do you understand that, dammit?*"

"Yes."

"I am going there now, and if I have to shoot the *Guardia Civil* dead to do it, I am going to remove those mines. And if I blow them in the process, at least I will do it *trying*, god damn it! I am *not* going to sit by and watch those kids burn just so Cobra does not lose its funding!"

"I understand."

"So you can either help me, or you can do nothing, and let me and the kids die! *What's it going to be?*"

THIRTEEN

He spoke quietly.

"I have spoken to a contact in Gibraltar. He was with the Regiment. He has a device and is on his way to deliver it to you tonight. His name is Ewan."

My head was reeling. "I didn't expect that."

"Perhaps you should have. He'll be arriving at your hotel in about half an hour. Let him take your Lamborghini away, I think you've had quite enough excitement for one week, and he'll leave you a Land Rover Defender parked outside the hotel. You take that. You'll find some toys in the back."

"He's not coming to Cazorla?"

"No, he can't."

"It's not a one-man job."

"I'm afraid you'll have to do it on your own, Harry. There is nobody I can call on in the time we have."

It wasn't the first time I'd heard that, and I knew it probably wouldn't be the last. I nodded like he could see me and said simply, "OK." I was about to hang up but had a thought. "Sir, is anybody monitoring the *Princess Diana* in Cadiz?"

"Yes, partially. They are trying to monitor its communications from Gib, but there is a complete blackout. It's as though the ship had never docked. Spain is releasing not a word. But eyes in the area say it looks as though it is preparing to unload tonight."

"So we are on the clock."

"Yes."

I got back to the hotel and made it to my suite without passing through reception. I had time to shower and change my clothes, and collect the drone from my truck, before the concierge called to say there was someone in reception to see me.

When I got there, there was a guy waiting for me in a leather armchair, reading the paper. When I walked in he smiled like he knew me and stood. He had fair hair, a burgundy cravat and a green tweed jacket. He was like a clone of the brigadier, only twenty years younger.

"Harry," he said, reaching out his hand. "Good to see you. I was in the area and decided to drop in. I hope it's not inconvenient."

"Ewan, not at all. It's good to see you. I was actually going to go to Malaga for dinner. You want to join me?"

"Love to. We'll go in my car if you like, and I can drop you off on my way back."

I laughed. The guy was smooth. "Tell you what, Ewan. Maybe you can do me a favor."

"Anything, old chap."

"I have to return a Lamborghini I rented. That's actually the main reason I am going to Malaga—" I broke off and stepped over to the reception desk. "You want to have the boy bring up my Lamborghini? Thanks." I turned back to Ewan. "You take the Lambo and I'll take your Land Rover. How does that sound.?"

He laughed. "I'm not complaining!"

We did a bit of back slapping and stepped outside to wait for the car. After a moment the Hurracán growled up and the boy climbed out, leaving the engine running. I gave him ten bucks and he went away with a *"Gracias, señor!"*

Ewan laid his hand on my shoulder. "See you on the other side, old chap. Don't know where you're going or what you're going to do, but from the hardware I can hazard a guess. I wish you luck. I only wish I could come along for the ride."

"You're not alone in that."

He knew better than to ask questions. He nodded that he understood, then pointed to the sky in the northeast. "Weather's not with you, I'm afraid. You'll have rain and wind in Jaen." Without another word he climbed in the Lamborghini and thundered away down the Avenue toward the freeway. Two minutes later I took the same route.

He wasn't wrong about the weather. It was a three-and-a-half-hour drive through the dark. The first twenty minutes were along the coast, but at Malaga the road turned inland and I began to climb toward Granada. By the time I got there the sky was turning from dark turquoise to black under lowering clouds, and as I turned north into Jaen the clouds began to spit and release their heavy load. The higher I climbed the heavier grew the rain until my headlamps were illuminating nothing but streaking gold and silver needles, and visibility was down to barely fifteen or twenty feet.

The road began to weave and wind, gleaming wet black and silver. And all the while I was wondering what effect the rain was going to have on the bus. Was the earth under all that weight going to give way? Was it going to crumble? Was the drumming of the downpour going to destabilize the bus and send it crashing into the ravine, triggering the mines?

The road began to wind more steeply. Curves and corners became hairpin bends between black ravines, forcing me forever back on myself. Frustration became a physical thing that seemed to be pushing me back, driving me away from the kids in the bus. My foot grew heavy on the gas. I cut the corners, growing reckless. I told myself if any vehicle were coming the other way I'd see the lights in time. But in that downpour, at that time of the morning, only the crazy and the desperate would be out driving. And right then I was both.

By the time I finally reached Cazorla it was four in the morning. The roads were shallow rivers running with icy water. The houses and apartment blocks stood like shrouds with blind, dead eyes under the sheets of rain. In my mind I had an image of where the bus was, where the river ran through the ravine, and where the cops had their barriers set. I had seen it on the camera from the drone. But I had done no real recon. The details of the terrain were unknown to me. The course of the river, its cascades and rapids, and the exact place where I would need to start to climb, were all unknown.

The one thing that was drummed into you over and over in the Regiment was that bad preparation was tantamount to suicide. I had not prepared badly. I had simply not prepared at all. And this was the suicide mission to end all suicide missions.

I bypassed the town of Cazorla on the south, came off the blacktop, killed the lights on the truck and began to plough my way slowly along dirt tracks that had become bogs of potholes and mud. I ground past a mediaeval castle that loomed against the pale glow of the town, an evil silhouette against the bellying clouds, tinged orange by the lights of Cazorla. I kept going and eventually the rutted, muddy path opened out into a muddy esplanade beyond which a swollen river flowed noisily—a strong current rushing against rocks. A freezing current that was going to be against me all the way.

I sat and stared through the spattered windshield at the welling black water and the faintly luminous foam. I had not prepared for this. I had not prepared at all. But there was no turning back. There was no time. At any second the cliff could give way under the rain and the weight of the bus; or worse, the container in Cadiz could be unloaded and the timer could run down, detonating the bombs. I had absolutely no idea how long I had. It could be a day, or it could be seconds.

I could even now be out of time.

I climbed out of the cab and was instantly drenched in freezing rain. I wrenched open the trunk and pulled out a Carrefour shopping bag that seemed to be stuffed full of a small, camouflage rucksack. I clambered into the passenger seat, slammed the door to shut out the cold and the rain, and pulled the rucksack from the bag. I unzipped it. The most important item inside was the EMP. It was a foot-long rectangular plastic case, four inches deep and two or three inches across. From what I could make out it was composed of four big lithium batteries with a booster and a basic circuit where the discharge occurred. It wasn't light, but it was light enough. A brief note told me it had a range of six feet in each direction—so a total of twelve feet. That was enough. I knew the gas tank was less than twelve feet from the rear axle. The pulse was triggered either by a radio signal from a detonator which was included in the box, or by a red button on the case itself.

I sat back and rubbed my face, feeling suddenly drained. All I had to do was fly the drone up the mountainside and land it accurately in a pitch-black deluge that would have had Noah worried.

I rummaged deeper in the bag. There was also a collapsible crossbow with two dozen tranquilizer darts. According to the note each dart was good to put a grizzly to sleep in a matter of seconds. It was mounted with a laser-targeting device and a night-vision telescopic sight. There was also a set of night-vision goggles, and that was it. Santa had been and Christmas was over.

I sat and thought for a moment. It was pretty clear to me that the drone was not going to make it. In this downpour, if the water didn't leak into the electric circuits, the sheer weight of the rain would make it impossible to fly. Plus the visibility from the camera would be virtually nil. Which meant that the only way to place the EMP would be to climb the ravine and place it by hand under the rear axle of the bus, preferably without getting shot in the process. At least the weather was in my favor for that.

That done I would have to locate the *Guardia Civil*, put them to sleep, connect the bus's tow bar to the tractor with a chain, and tow the bus away from the ravine. Then get back to the Land Rover and return to the hotel in time for breakfast. No problem.

I stuffed the items back in the rucksack, swung down from the cab and slung the sack on my back. Then I crossed the ten feet of mud that separated me from the engorged river and waded in. The current was strong and by the time I was knee-deep it was practically sweeping my feet from under me. I figured the far shore was forty to fifty feet away, though it was hard to judge in the dark and the rain. I knew I had to cross here, because the coach was on the far side, and the higher I climbed up the ravine, the wilder the river was going to get. But I also knew that pretty soon the current was going to pull me off my feet and drag me downriver fast.

I didn't think too much, I plotted a rough course and plunged. I was cold already, but the shock was violent. Cazorla is pretty high up, it was the middle of winter and this water was a mix of icy rain and melting snow. For a moment I was paralyzed by the shock, but I kicked hard and struck out for the far side.

I managed a couple of strokes before the current at the center of the river grabbed me and dragged me, tumbling and spinning, downstream. I kicked and thrashed, and fought against the drag, but I might as well have whistled Dixie. I was fighting tons of water and losing.

Then an agonizing, stabbing pain pierced my back and shoulder as the water slammed me hard against a rock. My lungs seized and I clawed at the rock, unable to breathe. I knew if the water took me again I'd drown. I clung hard and after thirty agonizing seconds I was able to drag air into my lungs again. Though doing so felt like shards of glass were piercing my chest. I wondered briefly if I'd fractured a rib, but put the thought out of my mind. A fractured rib was not an option.

I looked back and figured I had crossed maybe twenty feet of water, and had been dragged forty or fifty downstream. I gave myself another minute to recover my breath, then, trying hard to ignore the pain, I struck out for the far bank. It wasn't easy. I knew I had damaged my back and my ribs. Shooting pains pierced my lungs, sending them into spasms, making it near impossible to use my arms. Movement toward the bank was slow, and with every kick of my legs I thought I was going to go under, swallowing water. By the time I felt the slimy mud under my feet, I had lost another sixty or seventy feet. I dragged myself, retching painfully and staggering, out of the swirling, dragging mire, into the freezing rain.

There I collapsed at the foot of a pine, shivering, with my teeth chattering, trying to breath steadily and feeling I had been defeated before I had even reached the fight.

After five long minutes I forced myself to my feet, hoisted the rucksack on my back and began the long, slow trek along the riverbank toward the gorge. Mountain riverbanks are not easy to follow. They are littered with rocks, boulders, trees and undergrowth. Every step is either a battle to get through reeds and bramble, or a long detour to get around them. And, the deeper you get into the ravine, the rocks become more of a problem.

Here the water cascaded and splashed in a freezing mist, drenching the rocks and the boulders, making them cold and slippery. And the steepness and the narrowness of the gorge meant I could no longer make detours to get around them. I had to climb, blinded by the rain falling from above, slipping and sliding on the slick, drenched stone. For every three steps I managed to haul myself up, I slipped one from the smooth, wet boulders, or in the loose mud and gravel. When that happened the unforgiving, unrelenting stones bit into my hands and fingers, and my legs, sending shafts of paralyzing pain through my limbs.

It was maybe three hundred yards along the riverbank, and a climb of maybe three hundred feet. In sunlight and warmth it would have been a cinch. In the freezing rain and the dark it took me over an hour and was one of the most painful, difficult things I had ever done. Eventually, after an eternity, I came to a rock shelf about six feet high. I took a grip of the ledge and dragged myself up, with the stones biting into my frozen fingers, and the shrubs and branches tearing at my chest, but when I finally reached the top and lay gasping in the mud, I saw ahead of me, just fifty or sixty feet away, the massive, black shadow of the coach, balanced like a bizarre seesaw on the edge of the ravine.

I lay motionless for a few seconds, listening, but all I could hear was the roar of the river below and the hiss of the rain in the trees and on the ground. I rolled on my belly and slipped the night-vision goggles over my eyes, and they exposed the world around me in eerie black and green luminescence.

The shape of the coach stood out, stark and sharp, against the background light from the town below. Its windows shimmered a strange lime green, and odd silhouettes appeared, bundled inside at the rear.

Over on my right I could now see the green, gleaming wet shapes of two Land Rovers, a tractor and a crane. Very slowly, and using irregular motion, I inched closer to the nearest Land Rover. Gradually I became aware of the figures of two men inside. By the position of their heads, slumped forward, I figured it was a safe bet they were asleep.

All my training and years of experience told me to proceed slowly and methodically. But in my head there was a voice yelling at me that the detonators could be counting down the last seconds while I lay here in the mud. I loaded six darts into the crossbow, got to my feet and moved at a crouching run behind the nearest truck and began to approach the second one.

Sometimes, very rarely, luck plays a part in a successful operation. And that night, just for a few seconds, I got lucky. Persistent cold and rain seem to have an effect on most people's bladders, and when I was just thirty yards from the truck, the door opened and a guy in a large, military green poncho climbed out, hunched his shoulders and ran for the shelter of the trees beside the truck. There he stopped and, in eerie black and green, adopted that universal posture, with his hands in front and his head looking down.

As soon as he was motionless I shot him in the back. I heard him curse, "*Hijo puta!*" He turned, trying to reach over his shoulder, took a couple of steps, went down on his knees and then slumped on his face. By that time I had re-cocked the crossbow and run a few paces forward. There I dropped on my belly and waited as the far door of the truck opened and the downed cop's partner came out at a run, calling "*Juan! Juan! Que te ha pasado, tío?*"

He wanted to know what had happened to his pal. He found out pretty fast. I shot him in the chest. I heard, "*Me cago en la leche!*" which is a pretty weird, untranslatable Spanish curse involving milk and bowel movements, and he lay down to sleep too.

The heavy downpour had muffled most of the noise, and I was pretty confident that the cops in the other Land Rover hadn't heard anything. But to be on the safe side I loped forward a few paces across the luminous green puddles, and peered through the window. They were both still in the land of Nod.

I had the option right then of opening the door and shooting them both while they slept. But there was a risk involved, of one of them getting away and raising the alarm while I was busy shooting the other. In a split second I decided against it. The absolute priority was to kill the detonators and get the kids at least partially out of danger.

I moved forward at a run till I came to the rear of the bus. It was raised about six feet above the ground and the rain drumming on the metal was making an unholy din. I checked the cap for the gas tank and saw the ugly mine beside it. Underneath the chassis, by the rear axle, I found the other. I figured they were about six feet apart, maybe less, estimated the midpoint and placed the EMP device on a rock at that point. My hands were numb and my fingers were wet and useless, but I pulled the detonator from my pocket, flexed my fingers and breathed on them, then placed my thumb on the red button.

FOURTEEN

THE SHOUT CAME OVER THE DRUMMING OF THE RAIN and the muted roar of the river below. I turned and saw the two cops I had not shot. It had been a judgment call and I had called it wrong. They were twenty feet away from me in their military green ponchos, training guns on me. One of them was pointing to the ground and shouting, *"Suelte el arma! Suelte el arma!"*

I figured he was telling me to let go of the weapon. I shouted back, *"EMP! Electro-Magnetic Pulse! EMP!"*

"Suelte el arma!"

This time there was an edge to his voice. He was telling me it was a final warning. I held up the device for them to see.

"E-M-P!" I said again. "Electro-Magnetic Pulse!" The damn words were Latin, they should understand them.

The nearest one stepped in close and snatched it from my hand. He showed it to his pal. *"Es un detonador!"* He thought it was a detonator.

"No, no no!" I shook my head, inventing Spanish as I went. *"Electro magnetico pulso! No detonator!"*

They started rattling in Spanish and through the tree line I saw glowing green headlamps approaching. They had alerted their superiors and within seconds this was going to be a barracks. I had no time.

And that was when the beeping started. Sharp, piercing, cutting through the roar of the rain and the river at one-second intervals.

I saw the *Guardias* frowning over my shoulder and swung round to look. A two-inch panel had lit up on the limpet mine. It was an LCD showing the numerals 18, and with every beep the number dropped. 17, 16...

I swore violently, leapt forward and snatched the EMP from the cop's hand. My own hands were still numb. My fingers felt like hurting pork sausages and the device jumped in my hands. I felt a fist smash into my shoulder and the device fell into the mud. I scrambled, reaching for it. The night-vision goggles slipped from my head and I felt a heavy body land on top of me. I glanced up at the mine, counting down the last seconds. 13, 12...

I turned savagely and smashed my elbow into the cop's head. He grunted and sagged, and became a dead, heavy weight on my legs. I reached for the EMP. My numb fingers touched it and it slithered in the mud and the rain, toward the edge of the precipice. I looked up. 10, 9, 8...

I roared and kicked and writhed, slammed my hand on the device, turning it over in my useless fingers, slithering in the mud, searching for the red button. It was slick with slime and water, impossible to get a firm hold on. I looked feverishly at the mine above my head. 5, 4, 3...

Time slowed. I knew I was in the presence of death—mass death. I turned the oblong box toward me. I heard a semiautomatic being cocked. I heard a bellowing voice. I saw the red numbers turn from 2 to 1 and 0 as I slammed my fist on the red detonator button.

There was utter stillness. I looked back at the wide-eyed cop kneeling, staring at me, holding his gun in both hands. I held up both my hands. I slithered toward him and when I was just four feet away I kicked him in the jaw. As he went down I scrambled to my feet and ran, slipping and falling as I went, toward the tractor.

Through the trees I could make out the headlamps approaching. I wiped the mud and the rain from my eyes as I reached the tractor. I was telling myself that if they had brought it here to pull the bus from the ravine, it must have a cable. I searched back and front, but found no cable. So I scrambled to the crane, clambered in and fired it up.

I rolled forward through the mud, with the powerful headlamps playing on the teetering bus, illuminating the shower of silver needles kicking up a sparkling spray all over it. When I was six feet from the rear, I jumped down. Now I could see faces plastered against the glass, pale and moonlike, staring out at me. I hauled the winch forward. It was like a razor cutting into my freezing hands, but I ignored the pain and hooked the heavy, steel cable onto the tow bar, then ran back and clambered into the cab.

I could see the lights converging on the gate, forcing their way into the esplanade. I could hear shouts and honking. I ignored it all. I knew I was probably going to get shot. But I didn't give a damn. In my mind I could see a little four-year-old girl in Helmand Province, in Afghanistan, who had died because I had not been able to act. And I knew that whatever happened, these kids in this bus would not die today.

I put the big machine in reverse. The cable went taut. There was a terrible, squealing, screeching noise of tortured steel that cut through the roar of the river and the hiss of the rain. The bus teetered from side to side, threatening to keel over. I pressed the gas harder. The caterpillars ground into the mud. The front of the bus swung wildly, first right, then left. I roared like some kind of demented daemon, like I could make the bus yield by sheer force of will. I floored the pedal. The huge diesel rattled and whined and suddenly the bus was wrenching backward, bouncing on the rocks and slithering in the mud, rolling back toward the crane.

Then suddenly there was a crackle. Lights flared in the darkness and a hail of lead pinged and rattled against the crane. I swore as rage welled inside me and I jumped down into the sludge. There were confused shouts and more hails of bullets. Somebody was shouting, *"Cuidado con los niños! Alto el fuego! Los niños!"*

Something about don't shoot, and the kids. It was good advice. I lay on my belly and writhed and wriggled through the mud toward the ravine, back the way I had come. There was a growing, burning ache in my shoulder. I knew what it was, and I needed to get back to the Land Rover, and get help before it was too late, before I bled out.

I reached the edge and slid over like a snake, scrambling down over the rocks, slipping and falling in the wet mud and the loose stones. The shrubs and bushes tore at my face as I rolled and fell. I hit a large rock and felt excruciating pain, like long shards of cruel glass being driven through my ribcage. I figured I had hit the same spot I'd hit in the river. I tried to stagger to my feet, lost my footing and fell again. But this time I did not hit a rock. Suddenly I was in space, in blackness, with a strange feeling of peace and stillness. Like I had all of eternity to linger there in open space.

Then I hit the freezing blackness of the water. I gasped at the violence of the cold and struggled for the surface. As I burst out my ears were assaulted by the hiss of the rain on the river, and the loud roar of the fast-approaching waterfall. I struggled against the current to try and make the bank, but my back was crippled and the pain in my shoulder was draining all my strength.

Next thing I felt large, smooth rocks slide underneath me and I was in midair again. I knew the chances were I was going to hit rocks at the bottom and die. I searched for a peaceful thought, just in case the Buddhists were right, and I thought of the kids in the bus being reunited with their parents in just a couple of hours maybe, or less.

And I hit the water again. I plunged down, deep. It didn't feel so cold anymore. It felt peaceful. The dense fluid held me and soothed me, and I knew then that I was dying. It didn't worry me. Life, I thought, with an internal smile, was a lot more dangerous than death. I spun slowly, rolled softly, felt reeds caress me, and then, the pitiless river disgorged me, spat me out onto the surface and stranded me in the sludge and the mud on its banks.

I lay like that for a while, with the rain washing me clean. Slowly I regained enough strength to climb first to my knees and then to my feet. I made my way the short distance to the Land Rover and climbed in to sit shivering behind the wheel, with my teeth chattering, and wondering if I would have the strength to drive the three and a half hours back to the hotel.

I didn't think so.

I found my cell in the glove compartment, sagged back in my seat and called the brigadier.

"Harry."

I spoke with my voice shuddering with the cold. "The limpets were on a timer. I deactivated them and pulled the bus from the ravine."

"Good work. Are you all right?"

"No. I have a couple of fractured ribs and I've been shot in the shoulder, and I think I have hypothermia."

"Where are you? Send me your location."

I managed to send him my location, but my eyes kept closing and darkness was seeping like black ink into my brain. I could see the raindrops amassing on the windshield. Through them I saw a fractured, insane, sodden landscape under a leaden, gunmetal sky, and the horizon tinged with dawning light. Somewhere the brigadier's voice was talking, but I didn't know what he was saying. I was in the river again, floating gently, softly, held gently in her liquid bosom, and this time she was keeping me.

I surfaced slowly, quietly, with sweet water in my mouth. I saw her, on the bank, standing in the hot, desert sand, watching me. I waved to her and called out that she was safe now. But she just watched me drift by, and I saw that she had her father's blood on her white dress.

I tried to ease back into the gentle sweetness of the water, its clean, crystal kindness, where nothing could reach me or touch me again, but the desert sun was so bright it would not let me sink back. Water leaked into my mouth from the stream, and it was good, but I wanted to squeeze my eyes tight and go back into the gentle darkness.

A little more water leaked in and made me choke and cough. A woman's voice, perhaps the river's voice, whispered, "We have to keep you hydrated."

I smiled. What better place to stay hydrated than a mountain river? But even as I thought it, I realized that it was not water I could feel on my skin but cool, crisp sheets. The chance to die had passed, I had missed it, and it was not the river whispering to me, but a flesh and blood woman.

Reluctantly I opened my eyes.

I was in a bedroom which I recognized. There was a lace curtain wafting gently, trailing a spider's web of shadows across the floor. Behind the curtain the windows were open and sunlight lay across the quilt on my bed in big, twisted warm squares. I tried to sit up, but somebody had left half a dozen scalpels in my chest and a spasm of pain contracted my chest and I had to lie back and breathe.

A voice over to my left said, "You're awake."

I turned and looked up. I recognized the auburn hair and the huge green eyes, and the deceptively exquisite body. Araminta Browne, the woman I had known as Alice White,[1] was standing in the door of the en suite bathroom holding a glass of water.

"Araminta," I said, and closed my eyes. "Am I dead? Did they send me to Hell?"

I felt the mattress sink as she sat on the bed, and opened my eyes. She was smiling but her eyes looked worried.

"Hell said you caused too much trouble and sent you back. How are you feeling?"

"I was floating in a river. It was sweet and peaceful, and this angel was trying to drown me with water. She kept saying, 'You have to keep hydrated.'"

---

1. See Cobra 6, *The Silent Blade*

"An angel, huh?"

"What are you doing here? And how long have I been unconscious."

"I'm here to answer your stupid questions, and you have been out for about nine hours."

"Help me up."

She took my arm and eased me into a sitting position. I became aware my shoulder was bandaged and so was my ribcage. I took the water from her and drained the glass. As I handed it back I asked her, "The children?"

"Safely reunited with their parents."

"The *Princess Diana*?"

"Started unloading shortly before dawn. Part of the cargo was taken by a small, Greek container ship, the *Hesperus*. The status of the children and the bus was not known at the time, so all we could do was observe and report."

"What is the situation now?"

"Diplomatic fireworks. General José Ferrer García wants to give you a medal and then shoot you. He doesn't know who you are or who you work for, but whoever you are, he wants to embrace you and kiss you and do all that stuff Latin guys do..."

"And then he wants to shoot me."

"Right. The Company is denying all knowledge, as are the Pentagon and the White House, and the brigadier is moving behind the scenes to blame some rogue agent, possibly Danish or Israeli."

"Nice. What about me?"

"You're a mess."

"I know that. But what about my injuries?"

"Always so witty. You got a graze on your shoulder from a rifle round. You probably thought you were dying but it was just a flesh wound. Your torso looks like you spent the night with a hundred and sixty pounds of sexually aroused razor wire. You are also a bruise."

"What?"

"You are not bruised. You do not have bruises. You *are* a bruise. Your whole torso is a bruise, all the way around. I don't know how you didn't die from the thousand cuts principle."

"I still might. So what about the cargo on the *Hesperus*? What are they doing about that?" She shook her head. I pressed her. "What's that supposed to mean?"

"As far as I know, it means they're letting it go. There is no plan, the prey is getting away, and the brigadier does not want to risk another agent on an operation nobody has had any time to prepare for."

"Bullshit."

"Your bruise says otherwise."

"Bullshit."

"Eloquent. The man has a way with words."

"This is the brigadier's house, right?"

"You recognized the bloodstained sheets?"

"Where is he?"

"On his way. He's bringing Lucille Ball with him."

I scowled. "Who?"

"The funniest woman in the world, laugh-a-minute, life and soul of the party, Colonel Jane Harris."

I grunted. "She's the director of operations."

"Don't sound so defensive, Harry. She can be director of operations and still be a...," she shrugged, "you know, person."

"When are they due to arrive?"

"Couple of hours."

I handed her the empty glass. "If they're both coming here it's because the brigadier plans to finish the job."

"Makes sense."

"Help me up."

"Are you out of your mind?"

"Probably. Quit being funny and help me up."

"*Why?*"

"Because I need a glass of whisky, God damn it! You want me to get better drinking water?"

"You need to *hydrate!* That means water. You need to heal that bruise, Harry! Your shoulder."

"Shut up. What I need is a shot of the Macallan and a steak. Now. Stop giving me a hard time and help me up."

"No!"

"Fine," I snarled at her. "I'll do it alone and fall down the stairs and it will be your fault!"

"Jesus!"

FIFTEEN

I REFUSED HER HELP AND WINCED MY WAY OUT OF THE bedroom, down the stairs and into the pool area at the back of the house. There I winced my way across the patio and lowered myself with care into a wrought-iron chair at a round table, set in the shade of four palm trees.

Shortly after that a man in a white jacket brought out a tray of coffee, the kind of brown bread you could build walls with, butter and a large jar of honey.

"*Señorita* Browne ask me to bring breakfast, but she say steak and Rioja is comin'."

"Thank *Señorita* Browne for me."

He nodded and smiled. "She is comin' now."

As I ate the bread and the honey, and drained cup after cup of the strong black coffee, I began to feel better, and to realize how hungry I was. And when Araminta appeared, preceded by the smell of charcoal-grilled steak, I realized I was still hungry.

I consumed the pure, first-class protein with ravenous concentration, and while that set about repairing just about every part of me, the rich, red Rioja eased my muscles and dulled the pain.

Araminta watched me in silence until I had finished.

"Better?" I grunted and nodded. "Ready to see sense?"

I shrugged and made a face that was all ambiguity. Shortly after that the man in the white jacket came out and furnished me with a bottle of ten year-old The Macallan and a cut crystal tumbler. I poured myself a generous measure and toasted and raised it toward my lips.

"*Uisge beatha,*" I said. "In Irish, *uisce beatha*, pronounced *ishka baha*. Water of life."

I pulled off half the glass and felt its healing effects ease through my body, from the roots of my hair to the soles of my toes.

Araminta leaned her elbows on the table. "You know how many drunk guys have told me that?"

"Too many. You need to go out with a better class of man." I closed my eyes and listened to the birds getting ready to go to bed: "Have you brushed your beak? You wait till your dad gets home with the worms..."

"Some guy who could quote Greek to you," I said into the darkness behind my eyelids. "Make erudite jokes."

"Wouldn't work." Her voice came to me across the sounds of the cooling evening, over the turquoise lapping of the pool. "I need a guy who is enough of a brute to make me feel safe. I don't want to be protecting my man all the time. Know what I mean? But a guy who is sensitive enough not to be making me feel inferior all the time..."

She went on like that for a while, but she was miles away, on the shore, and I was drifting away on my boat.

The next time I opened my eyes it was dark. The window was open and a strange translucence was drifting in, moonlight like mist, fingering the lace curtains, lying like blue Dali clocks on my quilt. There was no pain. I smiled and drifted back into deep sleep, leaving behind me the hum of an engine, the crunch of gravel, and the distant slam of a car door.

I awoke at eight thirty, with blood and fire on the horizon. I sat up carefully and was pleased to find that my shoulder hurt more than my ribs. I stood and took a moment. I was not going to wince, I was going to walk. Like a man.

I walked, not necessarily like a man, but I walked to the bathroom and managed to have a shower. After which I managed to dry myself off and get dressed.

The stairs to the ground floor were a challenge, but by that time I had decided that what I had heard during the night was the arrival of the brigadier and the colonel, and I needed to convince them that I was OK and fighting fit. So I filed away the pain for later consideration and made my way out to the pool. They were there, in the early sun, drinking coffee and eating toast and marmalade.

Araminta looked at me the way a woman looks at a pair of shoes that are OK but not quite right. The brigadier raised his eyebrows high and dabbed his mouth with his napkin, and the colonel watched me with no expression at all.

"Good morning," I said, trying to breathe normally.

The man with the white jacket appeared as I sat and I told him eggs and bacon, and black coffee.

"Harry." It was the brigadier. "I didn't expect to see you up."

"Why not?"

"You're shot, and I believe you have three fractured ribs."

"I'm not shot. It's a flesh wound. Fractured ribs heal. I'm fine."

Araminta sighed loudly. "Harry, yesterday you were a wreck and you know it. When I found you in Cazorla you were practically drowned."

"I was tired. I've rested, and hydrated." I looked at the colonel. "Hydration is important," I told her and turned back to Araminta. "I'm fine."

The colonel leaned back in her chair. "I hope you're not expecting to go after Omeya."

Araminta poured me a cup of coffee and handed it to me. I sipped while watching the colonel over the rim of the cup.

"What makes you hope that?"

She sighed. I was making everyone sigh that morning. "Harry, what you did saving those children was extraordinary."

I felt a sudden rush of anger and frustration. "Don't patronize me, Colonel. It had to be done and I did it. If the general had been open to dialogue we could have told him what to do and none of this would have been necessary. But that's not the way it played out. The Omeya job was aborted temporarily, but now I am guessing it's back on. So I am going to finish my job."

"You are in no shape."

"How would you know?"

Exasperation made her eyes bright. "It's obvious!"

"No." I shook my head. "I mean how would *you* know? You have had no involvement in this operation, or with me as an operative. All you know about what happened in Cazorla is what you have heard. The brigadier has been in constant contact with me at every step of the operation, and Araminta came to Cazorla to get me. *They* know what shape I am in. All you know is what you've been told. And I am telling you I am fine."

Her cheeks were flushed pink and her eyes were bright and moist. The brigadier cleared his throat. I turned to him.

"Sir, we are running out of time. I am figuring the *Princess Diana* has already unloaded and the stolen container has already started its onward journey aboard the *Hesperus*. I know Omeya, I have a feel for him now, and I also know his wife, Rafaela."

He had started shaking his head before I had finished. "This is not a one-man job, Harry. Far less an injured man. This is a job for Delta Force. My advice to the Pentagon..."

I interrupted him. "Have you already spoken to them?"

He paused. His eyebrow told me he was not used to being interrupted, and he didn't plan to get used to it any time soon.

"No, not yet. As I was saying, my advice to the Pentagon is to send a Delta team to intercept the ship between the Balearic Islands and Sardinia."

"And we return our fee?" He didn't answer. That was none of

my business. I said, "How many contracts has Cobra failed to fulfill?"

It was the colonel who answered. "None."

"Until now. So this will be a precedent." Nobody answered. "So next time we fail to fulfill a contract we'll know the protocol. And the time after that, and the next."

I didn't feel real popular right then, but I didn't give a damn. The man in the white jacket brought me eggs and bacon and set it down in front of me. He poured me fresh, hot coffee and withdrew.

I ate for a while in silence. Then wiped my mouth on the back of my sleeve and sat back.

"I don't think it's a good precedent, and that isn't a protocol I am interested in learning. Fine, have Delta take the container ship with the Tic-Tac on it. But I am taking Omeya down, whether it's on his yacht in the Med, or at his first port of call. Do we know where he's going?"

The brigadier nodded, but the colonel spoke before he did. "The material you sent on the pen drive was useful. It was heavily encrypted and we are still working on deciphering it, but we have managed to work out that the Tic-Tac, as you call it, is on its way to the Black Sea. Omeya seems to be following the same route, just a couple of miles ahead of the container."

"The *Princess Diana*?"

"No, she returned to New York. The Groom Lake container was offloaded onto the *Hesperus*, which is, as we speak, following Omeya's *Azahara* east across the Mediterranean. They will pass Formentera and Ibiza this afternoon."

"The *Azahara* is about two miles ahead of the *Hesperus*?"

"Yes."

Araminta suddenly flopped back in her chair and laughed. It wasn't an amused laugh.

"Are we all going out of our minds? I feel like I stepped through the looking glass into *Alice in Testosterone Mania*. You have an injured shoulder and three fractured ribs, plus every muscle in your chest is bruised. Bruised means hemorrhaging. You know, that's what a bruise is, right?

"And however tough and macho you may be, Harry, these are the guys who hijacked a truck from a team of elite, Delta operators." She sat forward and thrust her face at me. "They-will-kill-you."

"Yeah? I am not going to parachute onto the top deck of the *Azahara* with a target painted on my chest. But with or without Cobra's sanction and support, I am going to kill Omeya." She rolled her eyes, opened her mouth and spread her hands. I interrupted her before she could speak. "The bruises—the hemorrhages—the lacerations and the exhaustion? I had all of those *before* I removed the bombs and pulled the bus back from the ravine." She closed her mouth and sagged. "I know my limits. I can do this."

The brigadier said, "All right. So what's your plan, Harry?"

I picked up my coffee cup and studied the black liquid. I was making movies in my head about how the whole thing would play out.

"As Araminta pointed out, I can't just board the yacht and kick everybody overboard. I'll have to wait for him at his first port of call. Making it look like an accident, at this stage, will be hard, not to say impossible, but I *can* make it look like the Russian Mafia."

"How?"

"I make the hit in Turkey or in Russia, or on the Black Sea. I know the techniques they like to use. They like to include some kind of punishment, make it look brutal. And, at the risk of being obvious, I could leave a message."

"The merchandise is probably for a Russian client. If it's not, it's either at auction or passing real close to Russia to reach somebody else. In any one of those scenarios it's easy to imagine how the Russians could get mad. So if Delta move in to 'rescue' the container, and Omeya is subsequently executed and his yacht blown to kingdom come in the Black Sea, that puts Russia pretty squarely in the frame." I turned to Araminta. "No parachuting, no acrobatics."

The colonel said suddenly, "You should know that Rafaela is on the yacht with Baldomero." I nodded, once. She went on. "There is also the issue of confirming the kill. If you bomb or torpedo the yacht, how can you confirm the kill?"

"That's not a problem. I was told repeatedly that Omeya's favorite place on the yacht is beside the pool. That's his office. It's where he conducts all his business, while his secretary, Anja, uses the real office."

"So?"

"So I need a powerboat and a drone, with one pound of C4."

She arched an eyebrow. "A drone?"

"I need the DRL Racer X. It has a top speed just shy of one hundred and eighty miles per hour. It has two Tattu Lithium Polymer batteries that develop four thousand six hundred RPM in each of four rotors, giving it a huge lift to weight ratio. It weighs less than two pounds, so it can carry a pound of C4 and a high-resolution camera with laser targeting with no problem. I'll keep my distance in the speedboat, approach at a couple of thousand feet, where the drone will be invisible and silent, and then dive at close to two hundred miles an hour, that's what—two hundred and ninety feet per second?—straight into his fat gut. He'll never see it coming. Hell, if he becomes aware of it at three or four hundred yards, which he won't, he'll have four seconds to react. And two of those seconds will get used up going, 'Eh? What the...?'"

She smiled and the brigadier chuckled. He said, "It's actually not a bad plan."

"It's a damned good plan," I said. "All you need to do is get me to Istanbul in the next forty-eight hours, arrange for the drone, the C4 and the targeting device to be waiting for me at the hotel. And I'll need a very fast launch. As soon as I see the *Azahara* arrive, and then leave, whichever way she goes, I'll go after her and do the job."

Araminta raised her hands. "Wait a minute! First of all, there is no way you can be sure that Omeya will be on deck when you put your drone up. Second, if you put a drone up that is going to stay in the air for twenty or thirty minutes, spying on the yacht while you wait for him to go to his place by the pool, then you are talking about a very different kind of drone, one with a maximum speed of thirty-five or forty-five miles per hour, not a hundred and eighty. Those racing drones have a flight time of two or three minutes, no more. Third, would you like to explain to me how you are going to fly the drone and pilot your launch at the same time?"

I sighed heavily. "Well, I guess, taking your questions in reverse order, you will pilot the launch while I pilot the drone, and the drone will have to be adapted."

She scratched her head. "Adapted? Racing drones have smaller batteries in order to reduce weight. You're talking about a max of one thousand eight hundred milliampere per hour. We can jack that up with Mavic 3 batteries at five thousand milliampere per hour, but it means the battery will be heavier and the drone will be slower. Still, with a reserve power source, and disposable..."

The colonel interrupted her. "Can it be done?"

"Oh yeah, now that I'm onboard, sure. It can be done."

SIXTEEN

10:15 AM TUESDAY 12-14-2021, ISTANBUL, TURKEY

We had touched down at Istanbul International Airport at noon on Monday, having taken the weekend to recover some of my strength after the night in Cazorla. We collected a rental Range Rover and drove into town. Cobra had booked us into a matrimonial suite at the 10 Karakoy, a luxurious boutique hotel where I had stayed once before, all brown and beige marble, near the Golden Horn.[1]

We'd checked in as Mr. and Mrs. Smith, collected the package that was awaiting us there, had the bellhop take our bags up to the suite and gave him fifty bucks to bring up a bottle of ice-cold Dom Pérignon and a dozen oysters. It was important, we'd agreed, to have a believable cover.

In the afternoon we'd confirmed the booking of the power launch—a Donzi 38ZRC capable of one hundred and four knots, that's a hundred and twenty miles per hour—and taken her out for a spin on the Black Sea. There I had assembled the drone and put her through her paces. I took her as high as three thousand

---

1. See Cobra 8, *Breath of Hell*

feet, where she was invisible to the naked eye, and we clocked her at about a hundred miles per hour in a near vertical dive. She'd do.

In the evening we'd had a quiet dinner in the hotel and retired early to sleep.

Now it was Tuesday morning and I was down in the lobby waiting for Araminta. My cell rang and the screen told me it was the brigadier. I stepped out onto the street where the noise and the bustle would make eavesdropping impossible, and said, "Good morning. What's the word?"

"We have confirmed satellite images of the *Azahara* crossing the Bosphorus at dawn this morning, headed for Istanbul. She seems to have overtaken the *Hesperus* and is making for the Ataköy Marina. You are familiar with the area, if I am not mistaken.[2]"

"You're not mistaken. I am familiar with the area. We'll take a drive down to the marina and see if we can get a visual."

"Be careful, Harry. If they recognize you…"

"Yeah, this is one grandmother who knows how to suck eggs, sir."

"I am certain you do. But it's not just Rafaela and Omeya, Harry. His security team got a pretty good look at you too, as did his secretary." The last carried a heavy hint of irony.

"I hear you, sir."

"Good."

I went inside and saw, simultaneously, Araminta stepping out of the elevator, and a man in a light blue suit talking to the receptionist. He looked vaguely familiar and something told me I didn't want him to see me. So I waved to Araminta and stepped outside again. She joined me a moment later.

"What was that about?"

"The guy in the blue suit talking to reception."

"What about him?"

---

2. See Cobra 8, *Breath of Hell*

The Range Rover bleeped and we climbed in and slammed the doors.

"I recognized him, but I can't remember where from."

She stared at me a moment while I fired up the truck and pulled out of the parking lot. "You saw his face?"

I smiled at her. "No."

"I didn't think so. He was standing with his back to you. So...?"

"I don't know. Maybe it was someone I saw from behind. The way he stands..." I shook my head. "I can't place him right now."

We cruised through the crowded, honking streets of the city, dodging, stopping and starting and weaving our way through traffic that was consistent only in the fact that it was chaotic and the drivers didn't give a damn about the rules. That was something I couldn't argue with. There was a bright sun in a perfect blue sky, but the air was cold and the sea, as we approached the coast, looked deceptively inviting.

We left the car in the parking lot of the Ataköy Marina and made our way to a nearby terraced café with a view of the port. There we sat and had a late breakfast and drank coffee.

At eleven forty-five AM the *Azahara* nosed her way into the marina and docked about two hundred yards from where we were sitting.

Araminta watched it while I sipped coffee and shifted my seat so I was looking at her and she could watch the yacht over my shoulder.

"So, tell me again," she said, "you promised this girl, Karina, a party involving cocaine and champagne in Omeya's office." I sighed but she didn't take the hint. "However, in that office you found Omeya's Aryan secretary. You tied and gagged both women with their feminine undergarments, stole the files from the computer and then fled the scene by jumping overboard and stealing a car, having beaten the driver and his pal to death with your fists."

"You left out all the good parts."

"You know, you get mad at Jane, but you are exactly the way she describes you. You're an animal."

"She's a good judge of character. What's happening on the yacht?"

"Nothing so far. So, I always had this idea she had a thing for you. You know the way we are sometimes drawn to what we most hate?"

"Pop psychology. Can you keep your mind on the job, please?"

"I always thought pop psychology was really accurate. You know, men are from Mars, women are from Venus, men need to solve problems, women need to be told you love them? That is just so accurate." She frowned and looked past me. "OK, big guy, big belly, on the deck by the pool. I am just going to check my messages..."

She pulled her phone from her jacket, positioned it like she was reading her messages and shielding the screen from the sun, and took a series of pictures which she sent to me.

I looked at them. "That's Omeya. That's his spot."

"We could take him now, in the port."

"Risk of collateral."

"Not if I was doing the flying."

"Cut it out, we stick to the plan. Can you see anyone else?"

She stretched her arms, lifted her sunglasses onto her head and laughed like I'd said something hilarious.

"No, no one. Oh wait—" She twisted around to call the waiter. "Get me a cold beer, will you? Beer? Cold?" She shuddered to show him what she meant by cold. He smiled, bowed and went away. She leaned forward with both elbows on the table, grinning, and said, "There's a real looker on deck. She's leaning on the gunwale and I would swear she's burning a hole in the back of your head with her eyes."

"A looker?"

"Real Spanish: death, sex, bulls, heat, dust—"

"I get the idea."

"It's all there, smoldering in that cute little body, the black bun and the Prada sunglasses."

"That'll be Rafaela."

"OK, so we have eyes, what now?"

I pulled out my cell and dialed. A moment later the colonel came on the line.

"Yes."

I grinned at Araminta. "Hey darling, how's it going? Are you doing your homework and helping Mommy?"

"What is it, Harry?"

I let a few seconds pass, like I was listening, then said, "Yeah, we've seen them both... Here, at the Ataköy Marina."

"Can you confirm Baldomero Omeya and Rafaela Omeya are both onboard the *Azahara* at the Ataköy Marina in Istanbul?"

"You bet, honey. Now, I need you to tell Grandad something, OK?"

"What?"

"I need you to tell him that I want him to keep an eye on them, OK? And look after them real good. And if anything happens, or they begin to move or anything, I want him to call me right away. You understand that, baby?"

"We have a team on their way already. You'll be notified the moment the yacht pulls out."

"You're a very good girl. Now, before you go, sweetheart, have you been studying the poem I gave you?"

"What are you talking about, Harry?"

"The *Hesperus*, the *Wreck of the Hesperus*, remember? Now what can you tell me about that?"

"The Delta team were about to take them in the Med, but the brigadier was worried it would alert Omeya. He wants the two attacks to be simultaneous. So we are waiting on you."

"Who is a *very* clever girl. As soon as Daddy gets home he's going to give you a very special present and a big ol' kiss."

"Have you anything more to report, Harry?"

"Nope."

"We'll be in touch."

"Bye-bye, darling, byeee."

Araminta had watched me throughout. When I hung up she said, "It's effective. You do it very well. But you don't do it because it's effective, do you?"

I shook my head. "No."

"You do it because you know it annoys them."

"It doesn't annoy the brigadier. It embarrasses him. It pisses the hell out of the colonel, though."

"You're really mad at her, huh?"

I pulled down the corners of my mouth and shook my head. "Not anymore. She can go to hell."

She spread her hands. "See? Women are from Venus, men are from Mars. Pop psychology. One guy saves another guy's life, and they're pals to the death. Simple. A guy saves a woman's life and he opens a can of neurotic worms. Things get *complicated*. It's a nightmare."

"So what planet are you from?"

"Betelgeuse."

"Thank God. C'mon, let's go get lunch."

"She's leaving the yacht. You want to tail her?"

I paused for just a moment, then shook my head. "Not worth it. Let's not complicate things more than necessary. We relax today, have dinner, finish the job tomorrow and go home."

"Agreed."

We took it easy going back. Araminta drove and I relaxed in the passenger seat. A couple of times I saw her frown at the mirror, but when I asked what it was she just shrugged.

"Probably nothing. Couple of times a car seemed to be on our tail."

"Same car?"

"No, first one, then another. Probably nothing. Nobody knows we're here, right?"

I ran through the list of people who knew we were in Istanbul. It was short. I ran through the list of people who *might* know we were in Istanbul. It was slightly longer.

"Omeya might have gambled we would follow him."

"Yeah." She nodded. "What are your plans for after lunch? You going to have a sleep?"

"I never mix work with pleasure, Araminta. You should know that."

"And you know that I know that that's a lie. We also both know you wouldn't go one round with me in the state you're in. So focus. You have a lie down to recover your strength for tomorrow. I'm going to go for a walk and discover this amazing, ancient, historic city, and while I am at it, see if anyone is following us. You going to be OK on your own?"

"I think so, Mom."

We had lunch at a terraced restaurant we found on the way, and got back to the hotel at shortly after three PM. In the parking lot I told her, "Let me go in first, see if the blue suit's there."

She nodded. "You go ahead. I'm going to take a walk around. See if I can find anything interesting."

"OK, I'll let you know." I paused. "Might be nothing, but it seems like a lot of 'might be nothings.'"

"Agreed."

We climbed out. I watched her make her way out onto the broad avenue, and pushed into the hotel lobby. I glanced around and found it empty, but as I made my way toward the elevator the concierge called me.

"Oh, Mr. Smith!" I stopped and approached the desk. "Mr. Smith, am I right that you have come from Malaga, in Spain? If so, you have somebody here to see you."

I gave a small laugh. "Somebody to see me? Our holiday was supposed to be secret. Did they say who they were?"

"Well, he said it was very urgent, otherwise I would have sent him away. He said if you were the Mr. Smith who was at the Puente Romano in Marbella, it was most urgent that he see you."

The Puente Romano. That was when it clicked into place.

The man I had recognized, and had last seen with his back to me, crossing the dining room.

"You did the right thing. Where is he?"

"In the bar, Coronel Sanchez Martinez."

The bar was like all cocktail bars in expensive hotels. It had wood-paneled walls, subdued lighting and lots of potted palms you could hide behind. I found Coronel Sanchez Martinez sitting behind one such palm with a glass of beer in front of him. He had his hands clenched in front of him like he was praying, but his expression said he didn't have much hope his prayers would be answered any time soon. When he saw me approach he nodded like a disappointed father.

"Mr. Redid, or is it Mr. Smith?"

"That depends on whether you know my wife or not." I pulled out the chair and sat. "Mr. Reid is in Marbella on a business trip. Mr. Smith is in Istanbul with his secretary, who is also called Mrs. Smith. Do I need to paint a picture?"

The waiter approached and I told him a dry martini. When he'd gone I said,

"I haven't much time, Colonel. What's this about?"

"Mr. Reid, where were you on the night of the 10th December?" I frowned and he added, "Last Saturday."

"Oh, right. I was at a party in Puerto Banus, on Baldomero Omeya's yacht."

"The one that is currently moored here in Istanbul?"

"Is it? I wouldn't know. Colonel, how did you know I was here?"

"Where did you go after the party, Mr. Reid?"

"Uh-uh." I shook my head. "You have no jurisdiction here, Colonel. This isn't even the European Union, let alone Spain or Andalusia. You want me to cooperate, you'll have to cooperate with me too."

He nodded and made a face like I'd said something interesting.

"Cooperate on what, Mr. Reid?"

"You want to know where I went after the party. No problem. All you need to do is tell me how you knew I was in Istanbul."

He took a pull on his beer, smacked his lips and set the glass down.

"Rafaela Omeya was assaulted by two men outside the Buddhist temple in Benalmádena."

"I know, I was there."

"You were there. You were very gallant and you saved her. From that point forward we watched every move that you made."

"So you don't need to ask where I went after the party. You already know."

He gave his head a small, sad shake. "No, then we followed the Lamborghini. You avoided our agents. We found you again staying at a villa in Marbella, and soon after you flew to Istanbul. But now you are Mr. Smith."

"So what has any of this got to do with you?"

The man who drove your Lamborghini is an *officer*," he labored the word, "...of the British Government. He is stationed in Gibraltar. The house in which you were staying in Marbella is registered to one Brigadier Alexander Byrd, also an officer in the British army. Both have connections with the elite Special Air Service. So, I have told you. Now, Mr. Reid, please tell me, what were you doing in Spain, and where did you go on Saturday night after the party?"

SEVENTEEN

I considered my martini for a moment before answering, then spoke carefully.

"I in fact know both of these two men, in particular Brigadier Byrd, from the British Special Air Service. I was eight years in that regiment, Colonel, and that's where I met them both. As to the party on Omeya's yacht, it got a little rough for my taste. I stay in shape, I don't drink a lot and a certainly don't mess around with white powders. So when they started snorting coke and letting off pistols into the water, I left and went back to the hotel. When I got there Ewan had dropped in—"

"Ewan?"

"The man who took my Lamborghini."

He frowned. "Captain Charles Cavendish?"

I laughed. "Army nicknames, Colonel. The brigadier was Buddy Byrd, I was Yankee Doodle, Charles was Ewan. Anyway, he took the car to return it and I went to bed."

He drummed his fingers on the table and sighed at them, like they didn't drum the way they used to. My martini arrived. I sipped it and set the glass down carefully on the table. "I am going to do you a favor, Colonel. But I want something in exchange."

He raised his eyebrows and spread his hands in a gesture that was uniquely Latin. "Tell me what you want."

"Some years back, I was in Afghanistan and I witnessed the Taliban massacre of an entire village: the old folks, the men, the women, and all children—everybody. However bad you might imagine it, it was worse." I paused, looking out at the bright day beyond the smoked, plate-glass wall, but seeing only blood and sand. "The worst thing was the children." I said at last, "Something like that, the impotence of watching it and not being able to do anything to stop it, it stays with you all your life."

"I can imagine."

"When I saw that coach on the news, with all those kids trapped inside it, I noticed that the bus had a tow bar. There were cops, Land Rovers, fire engines, tractors... but nobody was towing that bus out of the ravine. There were thirty kids on that bus, and nobody was doing anything to pull them out. I wondered why."

He shook his head. "You don't understand..."

"No, Colonel, I do understand. That's the point I am trying to make. We both know why nobody dared to touch that bus. And we both know who put the bus there, balanced over the ravine. But here is something I know, that you and your superiors don't."

I waited, but he didn't say anything. So I went on. "There were no motion detectors on the mines." His face went rigid. "And there was no remote detonator either. There was just one detonator, and it was on an automatic timer, set to go off at the time the *Princess Diana* and the *Hesperus* left the port of Cadiz."

His skin turned sallow. "How can you know this?"

"That's not important now. What is important is that some bastard set those children up so that he could get his cargo through Cadiz and into the Black Sea without being stopped; so he could sell that cargo in Russia. But once that was done, once the cargo was beyond Spanish jurisdiction, those children, the teachers and the parents, were potential witnesses against him. So there was really no point in letting them go, in letting them live."

He sat and stared at me with furious eyes that threatened to brim with tears. I held his eye, and after a moment I went on.

"Now, what I can do for you, Colonel, is to tell you what I *would* have done, if I had not gone back to bed in the hotel that night. And in exchange, you will accept my explanation as final, and drop your investigation."

He gave me a nod that was barely perceptible.

"If I had had the courage, if I had not been so drunk and tired, I would have driven through the storm and the rain all the way to Cazorla, I would have parked down by the bend in the river, beyond the waterfall, I would have swum across and I would have climbed up the ravine to the place where the bus was stranded. There I would have used a crossbow and tranquilizer darts to put the cops out of action, I would have used an EMP—that's an electromagnetic pulse device—to defuse the bombs, and then I would have used a crane with caterpillars and a steel cable to drag the bus out of the ravine. After that, I would have vanished back downriver again."

"Like a ninja."

"Yeah, just like a ninja."

"And how many guards would you have shot with your tranquilizer darts?"

"Two out of four, and hope to get away before the other two woke up."

"It was a big risk. You could have killed those children."

"It would have been a risk, Colonel, if I had done it. Fortunately, I didn't. But I'll tell you what would have been an even bigger risk, and would not have paid off in the end. The biggest risk, the fatal risk, would have been following instructions and allowing the timer to count down, in the naïve belief that the children would be released."

He stared hard at his beer. "Whose instructions?"

"You know whose instructions, Colonel. The man whose wife, or daughter, you have been following. The man you followed to Istanbul, the man who is on his way to Russia right now to sell the goods that were stored on the *Princess Diana*."

"You can prove this?"

"Prove what, Colonel? I am just speculating and shooting the breeze. But if half of what they say about that man is true, you can chase him till the cows come home, and you will never catch him. Especially with his brother being who he is. These are the people who run the world." I sipped my martini and sighed. "We live in this illusion of democracy, but we all know that the decisions that count, the decisions that shape the destiny of our world, are the ones made by people like Baldomero Omeya," his eyes lit up for a moment, but I went right on, "Bill Gates, Jeff Bezos, Elon Musk, Mark Zuckerberg. They are untouchable, beyond our reach. That is why I left the army, because too many men who committed atrocities against humanity, ended up living large on the CIA's expense account."

"So you will not help me."

"I'll help you, Colonel. I'll save you a lot of trouble. The only way to get to these people is to trust in your god. Divine vengeance is the only way they will ever pay for their crimes." I smiled. "A bolt of lightning from a perfectly blue sky. No presidents to bail you out, no judges to bribe, just the guilty soul and God's divine wrath." He sighed heavily and stood. I looked up at him. "Keep watching the news, Colonel." I stood and held out my hand. "You did your job. The jury has deliberated. Now we must wait for God's judgment."

"God's judgment?"

I shrugged. "Well, I'm an atheist myself, Colonel. But each man to his own god, right?"

"You talk in riddles, Mr. Reid."

"Sometimes it's the only way to talk. You're a Catholic, right?"

"I am."

"So trust in your god, and keep watching the news. I can't say it plainer than that."

"Goodbye, Mr. Reid."

"Remember our deal."

He nodded and left without shaking my hand.

When he'd gone out of the lobby and into the bright, December sunshine, I called Araminta and stepped into the elevator. She answered as the doors slid closed.

"All clear?"

"All clear. Where are you?"

"Are you missing me?"

"Sure, there's a big empty space where your chatter used to be. Where are you?"

"Snooping. I'll be back in an hour or so."

"Fine. See you then."

I let myself into my room feeling suddenly exhausted. My ribs were aching and there was a constant, steady throb of pain from my shoulder. I stripped and climbed in the shower and stood under a steady stream of scalding water for five minutes, then switched to cold for another five, and finished off with warm water, lots of soap and shampoo.

I had pulled on my jeans and was toweling my hair dry in the bedroom when I heard the door open and click closed.

It was wrong.

She had said an hour or so. If she'd said that, that was what she'd meant. She didn't mean twenty minutes. Besides, she would have said something, some wisecrack as she came in. But there was just silence.

I stepped quietly to the clothes I'd discarded on the bed and pulled my P226 from my holster, then moved to the bedroom door and flattened myself against the wall. Whoever it was, was quiet, probably a pro, one of Omeya's men. I thought about Araminta and wondered if they'd got to her. I felt in my back pocket, found my cell, called her and muted it. So she'd hear me, but I wouldn't hear her.

The guy who came around the door was holding a matte black Desert Eagle. It looked like the .44 mag. He was pointing it at my head and if he'd pulled the trigger right then he would have blown my head clean off my shoulders. He was tall and gaunt and had very pale blue eyes. I knew him from Omeya's yacht, and by the way he smiled, he knew me too.

He said something that sounded like, "Hees roit he-yah, kep," but I figured what he meant was, "He's right here, Cap."

The Cap came and leaned on the doorjamb. He was the blue-eyed South African's bull-necked companion from the other night. He had the same crew-cut hair, but he was shorter and more massive across the shoulders. He had a neck like a tree trunk and small piggy eyes.

"Whadaya know," he said. "No naked ladies tied up around the joint this time?" He held out his hand. "Give me the Sig and I promise we'll make it quick."

I made the "Ya got me" face, held the P226 up, ejected the magazine and, having gained their confidence, smashed it hard down on Blue Eyes' wrists, just behind the butt of his Eagle while simultaneously levering the barrel back and up. I wrenched it out of his fingers and for good measure I leaned in and headbutted him before stepping back, dropping the Sig Sauer and grabbing the Eagle with both hands.

My victory was short lived. Blue Eyes hurled himself in a roll across the floor, pinned my legs in a rugby tackle and took me crashing to the floor. The pain in my chest and my shoulder was excruciating and had me paralyzed for two crucial seconds while the Cap vaulted the bed and pinned my wrist under his knee. Blue Eyes pounded his fist into my face twice and pulled a long, evil-looking blade from under his jacket.

My body hurt, my shoulder hurt and my brain hurt, but the sight of that long, razor-sharp blade made all the pain go away in a flash. I contracted my badly bruised torso and smashed my left fist into the Cap's balls, where he was kneeling on my right wrist. I didn't wait to see what the result would be. As his eyes bulged, I grabbed the collar of his shirt and dragged him savagely across my body and into his blue-eyed friend.

It wasn't the best tactical move I ever made. As he sprawled across me I had to scramble out from under two hundred and sixty pounds of muscle, but at least he was a temporary barrier between me and Blue Eyes' knife. As Blue Eyes staggered back, I kicked and thrashed, grabbed the bedside table and hauled myself up, knocking over the table and the lamp as I went.

Blue Eyes lunged at me, but he couldn't get his footing because the Cap was still between us, trying to get to his feet. I grabbed the lamp and shoved it in Blue Eyes' face, while kicking the Eagle hard with my heel, sending it skidding under the bed. He slashed at my face again. I weaved back, using the bed as support, grabbed his wrist in my right hand and hammered my left fist into his elbow joint three times while twisting his arm. He was strong, hard and apparently immune to pain, but when I stopped hammering and twisted with both hands he cursed, dropped the knife on the bed and bent double.

He wasn't done, though. He stamped at my shin and ankle and at the same time, the Cap, who was on his feet by now, swung a wide right hook at my head. I ducked, let go of Blue Eyes' wrist, grabbed the knife and rolled across the bed.

The Cap was staggering toward the door to grab the Sig and the loose magazine. That suited me. I made for it too and landed a good right lead into his nose. He didn't go down. These guys were as tough as boiled boot leather. He smashed a right hook into my face. I weaved back but it grazed me and it hurt. He followed up without hesitating with a cruel upper cut to my solar plexus and a cross to my chin which would have laid me out if I hadn't dodged it.

I did and hooked his right arm on my shoulder while I pounded five left hooks into his floating ribs. It was like punching concrete. I let him go, kicked him hard in the thigh with my heel and went for Blue Eyes again, who had the Sig magazine in his hand and was reaching for the pistol. I lashed out and kicked him in the face. He staggered back and dropped the magazine, but as I delivered a straight lead to his chin, confident I had at least one

down, he blocked it, crouched and pounded my belly four times
with some of the fastest fists I had ever seen.

The pain was impossible to describe, and to make it worse I
now wanted to vomit. He was sure he had me and took a second
to position himself for the killer blow to my head. It was a
mistake. I stepped forward and real fast I slammed the angle
between forefinger and thumb into his trachea. It didn't kill him,
but he thought he was dying. He clawed at his throat, turning a
nasty shade of blue. I turned, ready to take on the Cap, but he
lunged past me, limping, grabbed his pal and they bath ran for the
door.

I should have gone after them, and if I hadn't been half dead
myself I would have. But I had spent everything on that last blow
to Blue Eyes' throat, and all I could do then was stagger to the
minibar to look for a bottle of scotch.

EIGHTEEN

Ten minutes and two whiskies later, the door opened silently and Araminta came in on silent feet with her weapon held out in front of her in both hands. She looked me over for a second, then peered into the bedroom.

"There's a hunting knife on the floor," she said after a moment.

"And a .44 caliber Desert Eagle under the bed."

"Why?"

"Two of Omeya's men came to visit."

"How'd they know you were here?"

"We didn't get to chatting. They were too busy doing a damned fine job of trying to kill me. But remind me of something, you said when Rafaela came on deck that she was burning a hole in the back of my head."

"Yeah."

"But she was too far away to recognize me, especially from behind."

"Yeah."

"But she knew I was there."

She shook her head. "No, it just looked that way. She was looking over at the cafés and restaurants and it gave the impression she was looking at you. The way a painting seems to watch you."

"No." I shook my head. "I have been very stupid. She must have bugged me, my shoe, my wallet, something, when we were in Marbella."

"Son of a bitch."

"Omeya used her to keep tabs on me."

"We need to move."

I nodded. "Go get me some jeans, a shirt, pair of socks and a pair of boots. A jacket, a wallet. Take everything else, except my cell and my passport. Give it to the cleaners. Give 'em twenty bucks. That way it will look like I'm still in the hotel."

"Wait." She made a motion with her finger at her ear.

I shook my head. "No, it's not a bug. It has to be small, real small. Too small for a listening device. Book us into the Hilton—"

"Which one, there are like ten Hiltons in Istanbul."

I thought about it. "The Bakirkoy, on Kennedy Caddesi, it's less than a mile from the marina. We want the top floor so we can watch the yacht from the window or the balcony. We'll moor the launch at Zeyport, which is opposite the hotel."

She nodded. "OK, get your pants off." She went into the bedroom and emerged with my passport and my wallet which she tossed on my lap. "You keep your credit card, your driver's license and any ID. The rest we dump. You go over what you keep, your cell and your passport with a razor. I'm going to get a refuse sack from the cleaners. Then I'm going to get your clothes. Be ready to move in forty-five minutes."

THAT EVENING we were at the Bakirkoy Hilton, watching the *Azahara* through a telescope that Araminta had picked up while buying my clothes. She had also collected the Donzi and brought it around to the Zeyport. More precisely, I was lying on the bed trying to make my various aches and pains go away, and Araminta was sitting on the balcony eating a hamburger and watching the yacht.

"They're having dinner on the deck by the pool. He has his laptop with him, and his cell. We could do it now." I didn't answer and after a moment her voice sounded closer. "Harry."

I opened my eyes. She was leaning against the sliding, plate-glass door which stood open onto the balcony.

"I'm serious. What's to stop us. We're fifteen floors up, it's nighttime, there's all the noise of the avenue and the marina. We could strike now and be back in New York by tomorrow night."

I shook my head. "It's dark. There's too much risk of collateral damage."

"Bullshit. What you mean is you don't want to take out Rafaela."

"She's not the target. I want her to face charges. I don't want to kill her."

"She got to you, huh?"

"No. Besides, we need to coordinate with Delta, remember?"

"So I pick up the phone and tell the brigadier, we have a bead and we can strike now."

"No. I don't like it. What if we start a fire and it spreads to the fuel tank?"

She sighed and went back out on the balcony. I closed my eyes again and began to relax. Five minutes later I heard her voice again, tense, almost harsh.

"Get your ass in gear, Bauer. They're on the move."

I sat up and grabbed my cell. It rang once and the brigadier answered.

"They're on the move. We're going after them. Lock onto my GPS and have Delta coordinate with us."

"Roger. Be safe."

I grabbed the drone, clicked the pack of C4 into place with the detonator, slipped the Sig under my arm and pulled on my jacket. Five minutes later we were pulling out of the parking garage and speeding east down Kennedy Caddesi, the five hundred yards to the port, trying to look like we weren't in a hurry.

We left the Land Rover in the parking lot, clambered aboard the Donzi 38 and Araminta slid behind the wheel. The two massive seven-hundred-horsepower Mercury engines growled into life and we cruised out of the harbor like we were going for a leisurely, romantic ride under the moon.

As we pulled out into the Sea of Marmara, we spotted the large bulk of the *Azahara* emerging from the marina, less than a mile away. Araminta set a course toward her, but giving her a wide berth. We were just another boat in the narrow channel, headed neither toward her nor away from her. In the darkness we would be invisible aside from our lights, and on the radar we would be just a blip, moving steadily away.

She crossed our stern at about a quarter of a mile distant. We turned toward the coast, allowing her to pull away slightly, and finally fell in behind her when she was half a mile ahead of us.

I called the brigadier.

"Harry."

"We're on the prey, sir. Do I have the go-ahead?"

"Affirmative. Take him out."

The *Azahara* was doing eight knots in the busy waters, about nine or ten miles per hour, headed east toward the Bosphorus Straits. All we could see of her was her lights, but Araminta kept us discretely on her tail.

I unpacked the drone, checked it was functional, revved the engines and launched it. It hovered over the prow of the Donzi for a moment, and then sped off after the *Azahara*, closing the half-mile gap in just over thirty seconds, at a height of two thousand feet.

I held her steady and focused the camera, then closed in. I found Omeya, sitting at his dinner table by the pool, white table-cloth, candelabra and candles, and Rafaela in a floor-length gown sitting opposite him. I could strike now, and kill them both. It would be acceptable collateral damage, but something made me hesitate.

Araminta glanced at me, like she could read my thoughts. "What's the problem?"

I spoke without thinking. "There is other shipping in the area..."

"The target's Omeya, Harry! Not the damned captain!"

I sighed and swallowed, trying to still the burning in my gut. I said, "OK, I'm going in for the dive."

As I said it, Omeya stood. I swore. Araminta said, "What is it now? You want to switch? You drive, I take the drone."

"No! I can do it, dammit! He's on his feet."

"If he goes inside because of the cold we are screwed!"

"No, he's pouring himself a drink. He's saying something. She's laughing. He's sitting down. OK, I'm taking it down."

I dropped into a near vertical dive. Traveling at sixty miles per hour the dive would take between twenty and thirty seconds. The drone might become audible or visible one or two seconds out. They were both as good as dead. I watched as the targets grew larger on the visual display. I kept the crosshairs firmly on Omeya's chest. Five seconds and the drone was picking up speed, sixty-five miles per hour, seventy miles per hour, I was five seconds from the target. My belly was on fire. In my mind I was screaming at Rafaela to get up and move. In slow motion I saw her turn and squint up at me. A fraction of a second later, as time slowed down, I saw Omeya look up. Then he loomed massive, blurred, and half a mile away there was a brief flash of light, and a second later a loud bang.

Araminta spun the wheel, snapping, "OK, let's get out of here."

"No!" I grabbed the wheel, spun it back, holding the course steady. "We have to confirm the kill."

"*What?*"

"Do it! Hit the gas and we can be there in fifteen seconds. I confirm the kill, grab his laptop and his cell, thirty to forty seconds max, and we are out of there at a hundred and twenty MPH. Kill the lights and nobody will know we are coming, or leaving."

"Jesus, Harry!"

She hit full throttle and we surged forward, splitting the dark water into white foam. Within fifteen seconds we were right behind them. The yacht had drifted practically to a halt and people were scrambling everywhere, shouting to each other in Spanish. Araminta pulled up to the stern.

"You're out of your mind. They'll see us and shoot us!"

"Do you know what his laptop and cell are worth? Spoils of war, kiddo."

That made her pause. I scrambled onto the hood and jumped onto the rear boarding area. There was nobody in the saloon. I figured there was just the crew up on the top deck and Omeya and Rafaela. I ran. I pulled the Sig from under my arm as I sprinted up the stairs. By the time I had made the second flight that led to the pool area, I began to see people. A guy in white pants, a white shirt and a peaked cap ran down the stairs and stopped dead when he saw me. I didn't stop. I kept running like I belonged there and said, "*Donde va?*" which means something like, "*Where are you going?*"

He frowned like he was going to answer me, but I popped my left jab right on the tip of his chin and he went out like a light.

I reached the pool deck and saw a blackened, smoldering mess. The table was gone, bits of it were floating in the pool, along with bits of person. Some of which were recognizable as bits of Omeya. There were six people there; a couple of them in white pants and shirt were borderline hysterical. The other four were the Cap and his pal Blue Eyes, looking pretty rough, and two guys in leather jackets who I assumed were their security team.

There was no sign of Rafaela.

"Who the fuck are you?"

It was one of the two guys in leather jackets. He was six three if he was an inch, built like a barn door and mad as hell. I shot him through the right eye and then shot the guy next to him in the chest. They both sat down together like they were playing musical chairs.

The Cap and Blue Eyes were staring at me with their mouths sagging open. It was a fraction of a second. I didn't want to get into a firefight, and I knew Araminta had heard the shots and might be tempted to join the fray. So I sprinted. I plowed into the Cap and sent him staggering back. I ducked a big swing from Blue Eyes, shoved the Sig in his belly and blew his kidneys out his back. A long step across what was left of Omeya and I gathered his blackened laptop and cell phone from the poolside table. As I turned the Cap was leveling his semiautomatic at me. I dropped to the floor. His shot cracked over my head and I shot him in the knee. He let out a high-pitched scream and I put a second round through his jaw and out the top of his head.

Then I was running again, scrambling down the stairs to the saloon at the stern. I jumped into the launch and almost fell overboard as Araminta opened the throttle and we surged across the black water, back toward Zeyport.

With the wind and the spray in my face I called the brigadier again.

"Job's done. We're out of here. What's the status of the *Hesperus*?"

"Good. The *Hesperus* has been detained. It is now in the control of our friends and en route back toward Virginia. Go straight to the Ataturk Havalimani International Airport. There will be a private jet waiting there for you."

"Thank you, sir. We are on our way."

I hung up, flopped back and closed my eyes. Araminta said, "What'd he say?"

"He said there's a jet waiting for us at Ataturk International. Home, James!"

NINETEEN

I left Teterboro Airport as night was falling across New York. We had been flown to DC, where we had been driven straight to the Pentagon and delivered to a debriefing room. There we had spent two hours with the brigadier and some nameless officials who had gone over every detail of our story with a fine-toothed comb, before delivering us to a hotel where we were allowed to sleep and eat, but not talk to anybody. Finally, after twelve hours of sleeping and re-debriefing, Araminta had been driven off to Langley and I had been driven to the airport and packed on a flight to New Jersey.

Despite having slept at the hotel in DC, I had not rested, my body still ached badly and I desperately needed to sleep. I had hailed a cab and we were now cruising through the New York evening, easing down Lenox Avenue, enjoying the feeling of being back. I didn't notice when he turned in at 128th. I didn't even notice we had stopped till he said, "This is it, buddy."

.I handed over the money and pulled myself painfully out of the cab. I had no baggage, and climbed the twelve steps of my stoop to the front door on stiff legs with my hands thrust in my pockets. I let myself in and stood listening to the empty house and its stillness.

There was the spacious hallway, the elegant, broad mahogany staircase and the stained-glass window on the mezzanine landing. The double walnut doors onto the comfortable living room on the right. I had grown accustomed to it. It had come to feel like home.

I crossed the hall and pushed into the living room. The long dining table on the left, a darker shadow in the dark room. I switched on the light. The fireplace, cold and empty, gave the room a faint, homely smell of soot. The sofa under the bow window, the big armchairs, the books, the decanter of single malt and the cut crystal glasses, all of them were homely, comfortable reminders of my success.

My success as a killer.

The cold emptiness of the house, that was also a reminder of my success as a killer.

I poured myself a generous measure of whisky and sat in one of my large, calico armchairs, gazing out at the leafy street outside. After a moment I spoke aloud, and my voice almost shocked me in the silence.

"Boy, you're a real success, Harry. Look at everything you've achieved. A whole brownstone in Manhattan, an offshore account to hide all your money in, and a murderous heart as black as coal." I drained my glass and set it on the table beside my chair. "But hey, you're drinking the best whiskey from the best hand-cut crystal. So what do you care?"

I made my way to the kitchen, looked in the fridge and wondered about going out to a restaurant for dinner. I decided I was too tired to cook and too tired to go out. So instead I carried my bruised, aching body up the stairs to my bedroom.

Out of habit I checked my bedside table for my Fairbairn & Sykes fighting knife and my Sig Sauer P226. They were in the drawer where they belonged. My closest friends. My most loyal companions.

I thought of Araminta in DC. We had barely said goodbye. We had looked at each other for just a little too long, understanding the things we could never say. We had killed together. We had almost died together. But we could not talk together. She had turned and left. Maybe some day soon we would kill together again. Or perhaps not.

I heard the front doorbell. Out of simple habit I slipped the Sig into my waistband behind my back and made my way carefully down the stairs to open the door. On the way I had a flash of a conversation I had had with Araminta when I had first met her. Back then her name had been Alice. I had just moved into this house, and I suspected she was trying to entrap me or kill me for the CIA. She had told me I needed help. I had not fully understood then what she meant. I had shaken my head and told her I didn't.

I stood at the bottom of the stairs, remembering.

"Harry." She had paused, watching my face. "Please, let me be your friend."

She had been able to say that. I would not have been able to say that. I had said:

"There is no room, Alice. I told you. We sacrifice trust, and with it friends and family. There is no room for friendship in what we do."

She hadn't answered for a moment. She had put down her glass and stood. "That's very sad," she'd said. "I'm not sure it's worth it."

Then she'd pulled a card from her pocket and given it to me. "This is my private number."

I didn't go to the front door. I went into the living room and opened an old, wooden cigarette box. There were no cigarettes in it. There was just a card with a telephone number on it.

I dialed the number and it rang three times before Araminta's frowning voice came on the line.

"Harry?"

"Hey."

"What's up?"

"Nothing. I just wanted to hear your voice. How are you doing?"

"…OK… You OK?"

"Yeah, just tired, bruised. Listen—"

"What?"

"Long time ago you gave me this card, and asked me to let you be my friend."

"Is this some kind of joke, Harry?"

"No. No, it's not. I told you then there was no room."

"I remember. You were real sweet."

"Well, I'm calling because I wanted to tell you, I want to make room."

"You sure you're OK?"

"Yeah. I hoped you'd understand."

"I do. Thanks."

"Right. OK. Good night."

"G'night, Harry."

I hung up and became aware that the front door bell was ringing again. I stood and made my way across the living room and into the hall again. There I opened the door. There was no one on the stoop, but at the bottom of the stairs there was an indistinct figure in a dark coat. They looked up at me but with the dappled light from the trees and the shadows cast by the buildings I couldn't make out who it was. The figure began to climb the steps toward me, but I still could not make out the face. I felt a cold prickling on the back of my neck and a burn in my belly

On the top step she looked up. I whispered the name. "Rafaela…"

"You thought I was dead?"

A cold breeze dragged dead leaves along the sidewalk. The traffic sighed in the distance.

"I thought you were dead."

"You killed Baldo?"

"Yes."

"You didn't know I was on the deck with him." It wasn't a question. I didn't say anything. I just stared into her face. "Are you going to let me in?"

"Yes, yes of course. Come in."

I stood back. My head was aching and dull. I kept telling myself how beautiful she looked. I kept going over in my mind how she had been sitting just a few feet away from Omeya when the drone struck and exploded. She brushed past me, then stood on tiptoe and kissed me softly on the mouth.

I closed the door and took her coat. I was frowning.

"How did you...?"

She placed the palm of her hand on my cheek. "You thought I was in Marbella."

I should tell her that wasn't true. I should tell her the truth. But I could not tell her the truth. I could not tell anyone the truth. I turned away and hung her coat. I felt her hands on my back, then her cheek pressed against me as her arms encircled my waist.

"Darling, you thought I was at home in Marbella. I know. I asked you for help, and you came to help me. It was a crazy plan, but brilliant crazy."

She pulled me round to face her again, held my face in her hands, stroking my cheeks with her thumbs and gazing into my eyes.

"I was going to stay in Marbella. It was not my plan to go with Papi. I never go with Papi on his trips. You must not feel bad. Always I stay at home." She pressed against me, put her arms around me and rested her head on my chest. "I don't know why this time Papi decided I must go with him to Russia. I know you thought I was in Marbella. I know you did this for me."

I held her gently. I could feel my own heart pounding in my chest. I said, quietly, "How did you...?"

When she looked up again into my face her eyes were expressionless, twin dark pools studying my face.

"I heard the buzz of the drone. I saw the lights from the yacht reflected off the body and the rotors. I jumped." Now she smiled. It was an inscrutable smile. "Just the way you jumped from the party." She straightened my collar, ran her hands over my chest. "Don't be afraid, Harry. I know you did it for me, so that I could be free. So that we could be free to be together. Will you make me a drink?"

She walked through the tall, walnut doors into the living room and paused to look around. I followed but stopped at the doors.

"I thought you were dead."

"Poor baby," she said, still looking around the room. "You must have been so afraid, so heartbroken." She turned to face me, tilted her head on one side. "Oh, baby. Don't be so upset. I know you didn't want to hurt me. Are you going to make me a drink? Come and sit with me, we'll light a fire and we can talk about our future." She smiled, then giggled. "I am a *very* rich woman now!"

She sat in one of the armchairs while I fixed her a gin and tonic and poured myself a stiff scotch. Then I hunkered down to build a fire. Finally I said, "It was not just a tracker, was it?"

She didn't answer. The flames licked up the sides of the logs and I turned to look at her. She was gazing down into her drink.

"Are you very angry with me?"

"No."

"I had never met a man like you."

"Did he tell you to do it?"

She nodded without looking at me. "At first, yes."

I stood and walked to the other armchair. "At first?"

"When I told him you had deliberately bumped into me at Puerto Banus. He told me to play along, to get to know you and find out what you wanted. But when I began to know you, after we had made love"—she raised her eyes to meet mine—"I could not betray you."

"The bug?"

"I spoke to his chief of security. An American. He was one of the men you killed on the yacht. I told him I wanted a device that was invisible, but that would allow me to listen to your conversations."

"It was your idea, not Baldomero's?"

"I was crazy. I wanted you for me, but I was sure you had lots of other women. I was crazy. I wanted you just for me. Please don't be angry with me."

"I'm not angry." I stood and went to the fire, staring down into the weaving flames. "But I don't understand. Where was the bug?"

"My father had access to all the latest military technology. The bug is not nano-technology, but it is close, and it goes on your SIM card."

"You put it there while I slept."

"Yes."

So you heard every telephone conversation I made."

"Yes, and I recorded them too."

I turned to face her. "What about ordinary conversations?"

"The chip activates the microphone on your cell, and transmits conversations that are within reach."

Her eyes were steady as she watched me. My mind was racing, trying to remember what she had heard, what I had said. She had heard all my conversations with the brigadier, with Araminta, with Ewan.

"I don't understand," I said. "Why did you go on the yacht if you knew...?"

"Because I knew why you were doing it, *cariño*. I knew you were doing it for us, to set me free, so that we could be together. I know you love me." She frowned. "You do love me, Harry, don't you?"

I nodded. "You know I do."

"You are so quiet, so serious. I thought you would be happy to see me."

"I am happy. I am in shock. I was sure you were dead." I paused, then, "Rafaela, how did you find my address?"

She smiled. "Poor Harry. I told you. The chip in your cell. I know everything about you, darling. You know everything about me. I know everything about you. We are so intimate!" She started to giggle. "We are so intimate. Who can be more intimate than us?"

"What happened after the drone hit your father?"

"I saw it coming and I knew it was from you. I knew it was coming, because I had heard you say you were going to send it. In our special way, you had been talking to me. So when I saw it was coming, I jumped. You know I am an athlete." She grinned. "I have shown you that before, eh, *pillo*? So I jumped into the sea. Then you came looking for me. I tried to call you, but there was so much noise and shooting, and then you left. You did not realize I was there."

She sipped her drink, thinking. "After you had gone, the crew pulled me on board again and we went into Istanbul. I called Papi's lawyers, they are sorting everything out, the company is mine, my uncle is the president..."

She stopped dead. I said, "Your uncle?"

She smiled shyly. "I am bad. You will have to punish me sometimes, Harry. Sometimes I am bad."

"Why did you tell me he was your husband."

She spread her hands and laughed. "You would not need to kill him if he was my father. Or, well, that is what I thought then. But if he is my husband, you need to get him out of the way so that you can have me. You do want to have me, don't you, Harry?"

"Yes." I said it woodenly, with my mind spinning and racing, trying to get a grip on the situation. I watched her face turn hard and her eyes narrow. "I almost died for you, Harry. I allowed you to kill my father so that we could be together. You have to want me."

"I do want you, I am just in shock. I didn't expect you." I gave a feeble laugh. "I have been shot, beaten, I have cracked my ribs..."

"You will run my father's company with me."

"Of course."

"We will be free. We will live like kings."

"Yes." I forced a smile.

"But, Harry, I want you to tell me about Araminta."

"What do you want to know? She's a colleague. We have worked together a couple of times."

"She is your lover."

"No."

"Don't lie to me. A man must have a lover sometimes. It is necessary for men. But he must not lie to his wife. We will be married. You will be my husband. You will own the business with me. But you must not lie to me. And you must kill Araminta."

I laughed. Exhaustion was draining my strength, and I felt like I had slipped into *Alice in Wonderland* meets the Cosa Nostra. "Don't be ridiculous," I said. "I am not going to kill Araminta. She's a friend."

"You will kill her."

Exhaustion was turning to irritation, and I was getting mad at myself that I didn't know how to get out of the situation. I drew breath to tell her we were done, and to leave, when she snapped, "She was coming to see you. Did you know that?"

"What?"

"Tonight, she was coming to see you."

"That's ridiculous. She's not even in New York."

She wagged a finger at me. "I am being tolerant, Harry, because I know you are hurt and tired. But you will have to learn that I expect honesty from you."

"Go to hell, Rafaela!"

She stood and strode out of the room. I heard the front door open and stood to follow her. When I got to the hall I saw three men in suits pushing in. Two of them had Araminta gripped by the arms, with a semiautomatic stuck in her back.

"Is this what you meant by being friends, jackass?"

I stared at Rafaela. "What the hell?" To Araminta I said, "I thought you were in DC?"

"I *was* in DC. I *live* in New York. But the colonel thought we were getting too close and told me to make my own way home. Then you called and I thought, screw the boss. So I came over and found Bernarda Alba here waiting with her friends."

"Enough!" It was Rafaela. She turned to the third guy and snapped, "*Dame tu arma!*"

He reached in his jacket and pulled out a Glock 19. He threaded a suppressor onto it and gave it to her. She handed it to me. "Kill her."

I took the weapon, staring at Rafaela like she was crazy. She kept talking.

"You know how much I am worth, Harry? I am worth five billion euros. Five thousand million euros. You know how much power I have now that Papi is dead? I am probably the most powerful woman in the world. When you shoot this bitch, you will be my king. All of that riches, all of that power, will be yours too. We will be kings of the world. Shoot her. She is nothing. Kill her now!"

I didn't hesitate. I put a bullet through her forehead.

That gave me three or four seconds while the boys were in shock. I shot the one who was holding the gun on Araminta first. His brains erupted out the back of his head all over my door. But before he had started to sag at the knees I had shot the other guy who was holding her. I left the third guy till last because I knew I had his gun. By the time I'd shot him barely three seconds had passed.

I looked down at Rafaela stretched out on the floor. She looked genuinely surprised. There was something deeply tragic about her. The possibility that I would not want her billions had been inconceivable to her. The possibility that happiness could lie anywhere other than in wealth and power was something she had never considered.

A nervous smile fluttered across Araminta's lips. "Wow," she said. "That was intense."

I held out my arms and she came to me. I kissed the top of her head and whispered in her ear, "I am going to call the brigadier and get a cleanup team here. Then you can explain to me again just exactly why you were coming to see me."

Don't miss BLOOD ON BALTHAZAR. The riveting sequel in the Harry Bauer Thriller series.

Scan the QR code below to purchase BLOOD ON BALTHAZAR.

Or go to: righthouse.com/blood-on-balthazar

NOTE: flip to the very end to read an exclusive sneak peak...

DON'T MISS ANYTHING!

If you want to stay up to date on all new releases in this series, with this author, or with any of our new deals, you can do so by joining our newsletters below.

In addition, you will immediately gain access to our entire *Right House VIP Library,* which includes many riveting Mystery and Thriller novels for your enjoyment!

righthouse.com/email

(Easy to unsubscribe. No spam. Ever.)

ALSO BY BLAKE BANNER

Up to date books can be found at:
www.righthouse.com/blake-banner

ROGUE THRILLERS
Gates of Hell (Book 1)
Hell's Fury (Book 2)

ALEX MASON THRILLERS
Odin (Book 1)
Ice Cold Spy (Book 2)
Mason's Law (Book 3)
Assets and Liabilities (Book 4)
Russian Roulette (Book 5)
Executive Order (Book 6)
Dead Man Talking (Book 7)
All The King's Men (Book 8)
Flashpoint (Book 9)
Brotherhood of the Goat (Book 10)
Dead Hot (Book 11)
Blood on Megiddo (Book 12)
Son of Hell (Book 13)

HARRY BAUER THRILLER SERIES
Dead of Night (Book 1)
Dying Breath (Book 2)
The Einstaat Brief (Book 3)
Quantum Kill (Book 4)
Immortal Hate (Book 5)
The Silent Blade (Book 6)
LA: Wild Justice (Book 7)

Breath of Hell (Book 8)
Invisible Evil (Book 9)
The Shadow of Ukupacha (Book 10)
Sweet Razor Cut (Book 11)
Blood of the Innocent (Book 12)
Blood on Balthazar (Book 13)
Simple Kill (Book 14)
Riding The Devil (Book 15)
The Unavenged (Book 16)
The Devil's Vengeance (Book 17)
Bloody Retribution (Book 18)
Rogue Kill (Book 19)
Blood for Blood (Book 20)

DEAD COLD MYSTERY SERIES
An Ace and a Pair (Book 1)
Two Bare Arms (Book 2)
Garden of the Damned (Book 3)
Let Us Prey (Book 4)
The Sins of the Father (Book 5)
Strange and Sinister Path (Book 6)
The Heart to Kill (Book 7)
Unnatural Murder (Book 8)
Fire from Heaven (Book 9)
To Kill Upon A Kiss (Book 10)
Murder Most Scottish (Book 11)
The Butcher of Whitechapel (Book 12)
Little Dead Riding Hood (Book 13)
Trick or Treat (Book 14)
Blood Into Wine (Book 15)
Jack In The Box (Book 16)
The Fall Moon (Book 17)
Blood In Babylon (Book 18)
Death In Dexter (Book 19)
Mustang Sally (Book 20)

A Christmas Killing (Book 21)
Mommy's Little Killer (Book 22)
Bleed Out (Book 23)
Dead and Buried (Book 24)
In Hot Blood (Book 25)
Fallen Angels (Book 26)
Knife Edge (Book 27)
Along Came A Spider (Book 28)
Cold Blood (Book 29)
Curtain Call (Book 30)

THE OMEGA SERIES
Dawn of the Hunter (Book 1)
Double Edged Blade (Book 2)
The Storm (Book 3)
The Hand of War (Book 4)
A Harvest of Blood (Book 5)
To Rule in Hell (Book 6)
Kill: One (Book 7)
Powder Burn (Book 8)
Kill: Two (Book 9)
Unleashed (Book 10)
The Omicron Kill (Book 11)
9mm Justice (Book 12)
Kill: Four (Book 13)
Death In Freedom (Book 14)
Endgame (Book 15)

ABOUT US

Right House is an independent publisher created by authors for readers. We specialize in Action, Thriller, Mystery, and Crime novels.

If you enjoyed this novel, then there is a good chance you will like what else we have to offer! Please stay up to date by using any of the links below.

Join our mailing lists to stay up to date -->
righthouse.com/email
Visit our website --> righthouse.com
Contact us --> contact@righthouse.com

 facebook.com/righthousebooks
 x.com/righthousebooks
 instagram.com/righthousebooks

EXCLUSIVE SNEAK PEAK OF...

BLOOD ON BALTHAZAR

CHAPTER 1

I parked in the shade of a spindly oak tree near the corner of East 35th and 3rd Avenue and sat for a moment looking at the green awning over the entrance to the fourteen-storey apartment block at number 166.

Jane, the colonel, had come to see me at home, in my brownstone on James Baldwin Place. The colonel was Cobra's woman in the CIA. Cobra knew she was with the Company, but the very top brass at the Company knew she was with Cobra. The last time we had met it had not been real friendly, so I was surprised to see her at my front door. In theory she was Head of Operations. In practice I always dealt with the brigadier. He'd been my commanding officer in the SAS and we understood each other. Besides, the colonel and I just didn't seem to work.

But there she was, sitting in my living room, in her navy blue suit and her nice legs, telling me that Jan van Hoek had to die. He was a very bad man. He was a mercenary and, in the last five years alone, he had organized and executed the massacre of over three thousand people—men, women, children, the elderly and sick—in three villages in the Republic of Cabinda-Itumba, on the west coast of Africa. He had even received a medal from President Cosmo Manuel for his bravery in participating personally in the massacres. Now he was in New York, in his apartment on the fourteenth floor of 166 East 35th Street. And he was alone. *Get in your car and go and kill him.*

I climbed out of my ancient Golf GTI and crossed the road. Jan van Hoek had been a mercenary for over twenty years. Even in his late forties he would be dangerous, but he would not be expecting me. It would be simple, straightforward.

I crossed the cool, dark marble lobby to the elevators and rode one of them to the fourteenth floor. I stepped out into the air-conditioned corridor, carpeted in red with pictures of vases of flowers on the walls, and walked to the last door on the right. His was the corner apartment.

The door was opened after about thirty seconds by a man in jeans and a vest who was talking over his shoulder while he chewed something. His chewing slowed as he looked at my eyes. When you've been in the business that long, you recognize a fellow killer. You smell them and your hackles rise.

"Yeah?"

"I think I have the wrong address."

He shook his head. "It's OK, she's leaving. Come on in."

Maybe I should have turned around and walked away, left it to somebody else. But something was wrong and I wanted to know what it was. I followed him inside, through a small entrance hall to a large living room-dining room with a large corner terrace beyond sliding glass doors.

The furnishings were minimalist, on bare parquet floors, and in a white, leather armchair there was a woman sitting staring at me. She had very black hair tied in a knot at the back of her neck and very dark eyes that watched me carefully as I came in. She had a small plastic bottle of water in her hand. It was almost empty. She took a swig, still watching me, and set it on the coffee table. Van Hoek said, "Adelina, can we finish this later? Let's eat tonight. I'll call you."

She sighed like she was losing patience with something and stood. She gave me another look—this one would have killed if it could have—and made her way into the hall, followed by Jan. On an impulse I pulled out my handkerchief, picked up the bottle and put it in my pocket. There was some harsh whispering and after a moment I heard the door close. A few seconds later Jan van Hoek stepped back into the living room and grinned.

"Hi, who did you say you were?" The accent was Dutch, maybe South African.

"I didn't. Are you Jan van Hoek?"

"Sure, what's it about?"

I'd brought the Maxim 9. Unlike a Sig with a suppressor attached, the Maxim fits into a holster under your arm. Perhaps I should have killed him there and then, according to instructions, but I'd been seen—and scrutinized—by an unknown woman, and when he was dead she was going to tell the cops I was the last person to see Jan alive. I didn't relish that idea.

I pulled the Maxim and showed it to him. "We're going to go for a ride. I don't want to kill you, Jan, we just need to talk about a few things. Provided we can reach an understanding, you go back to your life and you never hear from me again. Give me trouble and I'll shoot you stone dead right in the lobby or on the sidewalk. This is New York, Jan, nobody gives a damn and nobody wants to get involved."

"Who sent you?"

"Quit stalling, Jan. I'll tell you when we get where we're going. Meantime get your jacket, and make sure to bring your wallet, your driver's license and your phone." After a moment I asked him, "Do you smoke?"

He'd gone into the bedroom, but he leaned out of the door to frown at me.

"Yeah, why?"

"Bring your cigarettes and your lighter too."

When he emerged from the bedroom he was looking at me curiously. He was wondering why I'd allowed him to be alone in his bedroom, getting his jacket. He had obviously slipped his shoulder holster on with a semi-automatic under his arm, and he was wondering why I had allowed him to do that.

That was fine by me, because a man who has been abducted for the purpose of execution does not normally bring along his cigarettes and lighter, his billfold, his driver's license and his Glock 17. It wouldn't get me off the hook if Adelina fingered me, but it would put a big question mark in any investigator's mind.

I said, "We'll take your car."

"Yeah, sure, no problem." He gave something that would have liked to be a smile, but lacked any real will.

We took the elevator all the way down to the bowels of the building. I followed him through a spring-loaded door into the parking garage. It was dark and smelled of dirt, oil and carbon monoxide. He led me to a Mercedes convertible SL 63 Roadster and I told him, "Get behind the wheel." He did as I said and I got in beside him. "The Bronx, Soundview Park. Leave the car on O'Brien Avenue. You know where it is?"

"Clason Point, near the amphitheater."

"Let's go."

The tires screamed in the shadows as we spiraled toward the road. Once we were out in the sun, headed north on the FDR, he said, "Be straight with me. You gonna kill me?" He glanced at me, then back at the road.

"I told you that's not what this is about."

He was silent then till we'd crossed the eastern Boulevard Bridge and peeled off onto Bruckner Boulevard. Then he said, "So what *is* it about? Do you have to keep me in suspense like this?"

There was a tremor in his voice and I could see he was gripping the wheel tight. I smiled. "What makes you so sure it's an execution?"

"Hell!" He gestured at the Maxim in my lap. "A guy turns up at your house with a suppressed semi-automatic under his arm and says, 'We're going for a ride.' What are you going to think?" He glanced at me. "I mean, it's not a Glock or a Sig Sauer, like any normal person would carry. It's a fucking Maxim 9. They are designed for executions, man!"

I watched him for a while, asking myself why the hell I should make the bastard feel better. He turned into the broad expanse of Soundview Avenue, with its low, flat buildings painted gaudy yellow, dirty white and sickly gray, its steel tubing and chicken-wire fences and concrete yards.

"Who was the woman?"

He glanced at me. "What?"

I gave a small laugh and shook my head. "Why are you asking me 'What?' Jan. You heard the question. Who is she?"

He didn't answer. I said:

"You want me to shoot you in the knee? I can do it now or when we get to the park. I don't mind. I don't want this to get ugly, Jan. I want it to be simple, no blood, no pain, no screaming and weeping. But you start bullshitting me and things start to get very ugly very quickly. Don't do it."

He'd been shaking his head throughout. Now he said, "No, no, no... It's OK, I didn't mean... It's fine, it's fine."

"Who is she?"

"Oh, man," because of the accent he made it sound like *Oh, men,* but he meant *Oh, man.* "You put me in such a difficult situation—"

"We're not friends, Jan. Don't get intimate with me. We're not going to get drunk together and swap war stories. This is the third time I'm asking you and it will be the last. Who is she?"

He accelerated down Soundview and turned right at Patterson. There he took a deep breath, turned left into Beach Avenue and at the end, where it becomes a dirt track and they called it O'Brien Avenue, he stopped and killed the engine. For a moment he sat with his lower lip gripped between his teeth. Finally he said, quietly, "She's my daughter. She's the only good thing I ever did in my life. Please, please don't hurt her."

I searched his face for the tell. I didn't see it, but I said, "Bull-shit. I've studied your file, Jan. You don't have any kids."

"Of course I don't!" He rolled his eyes. "Not on paper! That's all a bloke like me needs, people knowing he has a daughter. She'd never stand a chance!" He stared at me for a moment, his face tight and his eyebrows high on his forehead. "She's illegitimate, a bastard."

"Who's her mother?"

"Mariana dos Santos, a Portuguese doctor. Most beautiful woman I had ever seen. She was everything I wasn't. I was twenty, she must have been thirty-something. We moved into the village with the Land Rovers and the guns, y'know? We knew the men were working for the Demos."

"Demos?"

"Cabinda-Itumba Democratic Liberation Front. CIDLF. Not a great acronym, but the red bastards rallied to it. She was there with the *Médecins Sans Frontières*. She was brave." He nodded several times, gazing out at the tangle of wild trees in the park. He grinned at me, looking along his eyes. "She came at me with a scalpel, boy. We had thirty men in Land Rovers armed with assault rifles, rounding everybody up into the main square, and she comes at me like a fucking wildcat, holding a scalpel. I'll tell you, I fell in love with her right there on the spot. I grabbed her, disarmed her, carried her into the hospital hut and took her right there. The one time, and she got pregnant. It was meant to be. God, the Universe, the Devil, whatever. It was meant."

"You raped her."

He shook his head, dismissed the notion out of hand. "Nah! She wanted it. Woman like that? What normal woman goes to fucking Cabinda-Itumba, in the middle of the jungle to work as a doctor? She was there looking for adventure. It was primal. We were meant to be together for those minutes. Man and woman in the jungle, making life, surrounded by fucking death."

"So you killed everyone in the village except her."

"I had a sergeant drive her back to Buco, and from there she was sent to the capital city of Cabinda."

"And back to Portugal?"

He became serious and shook his head. "Nah. Government held her there, in Cabinda. They said the child had been conceived in Cabinda-Itumba and should be born there."

"You pulled strings so she wouldn't leave."

He didn't answer. "When the child was born they told her she could leave, but the child had to stay and be raised as Cabindalese. So she stayed with her baby, for five years, but when the child was five years old, Mariana died. Dr. Mariana dos Santos. *Médecins Sans Frontières*. Heroine. Dead."

"You had her killed."

"Of course not! Why would I do that? I told her if she married me, recognized me as her husband and the father of her child, we could leave, make a life in Europe, the States, wherever she liked." He looked me in the eye. "You know what the ungrateful bitch did? She spat in my face. In the end I think she died of depression, trapped like a rat in that shithole."

"This was the woman you were in love with."

He glanced at me and there was insolence in his eyes. "Fuck you."

"Get out of the car."

He didn't do it straight away. He gave my face a once-over first. Maybe he was trying to work out whether I was going to kill him; maybe he was wondering if he could take me right there and then. The Maxim answered at least one of those questions and he climbed out of the car while I got out the other side.

There was a low, dilapidated wire fence separating the dirt track from the park. It was easy to step over and we moved in among the wild ferns, grass and saplings that made of the park something between a savannah and a jungle. We trudged across the two hundred yards of scrub that separated us from a fringe of woodland that framed the park along the mouth of the Bronx River. When we came to the footpath he stopped and looked at me. Something in his eyes told me he had decided I was going to kill him. I said, "Relax, will you? Down to the water's edge. The water interferes with listening devices. I'm being careful."

A spasm of irritation contracted his face. "What the fuck is this about?"

"Quit stalling and I'll tell you. Let's go, down to the water."

We picked our way through the trees to the big rocks that flanked the river. I moved down, close to the water edge, and pointed to a rock about six feet from me.

"Sit down." As he sat I said, "Before I tell you what this is about, I need you to confirm a couple of things for me."

"Like what?"

"Tell me about Tanda Matiaba, Caio and Chimbete."

His eyebrows shot up and his mouth sagged open in a smile. He gave a small laugh. "You're kidding me. What are you, Interpol or some shit?"

I smiled. "More like some shit. There are certain things a Western democratic government cannot be seen to do. We take care of those things while providing credible deniability to respectable governments. Remember Roosevelt? Speak softly but carry a big stick? We are the big stick, but we can't be seen to be."

To my surprise he laughed and said, "Son of a gun...you're recruiting me! I don't believe it! You're fucking recruiting me to do your fucking dirty work!" He threw back his head and laughed out loud. I continued to smile, but said nothing. If this made it easier, so be it. When he was done he nodded slowly three times, watching me.

"OK," he said, "I'll tell you about Tanda Matiaba, Caio and Chimbete, but let me warn you, a guy like me does not come cheap."

"Don't worry," I said. "Nobody pays higher rates than us."

CHAPTER 2

HE REACHED IN HIS POCKET AND PULLED OUT A PACK OF Camels. He shook one free and took it into his mouth straight from the pack, then lit up with an old, brass Zippo. He took a deep breath and blew out a long stream of smoke.

"You know." He said it as a statement, then glanced at me as though for confirmation. "Just because they changed the regime and pulled down the wall, didn't mean the Cold War was over. Right? The Cold War was never about Communism, or freedom. Like the Eagles said, freedom, that's just some people talking. It was about power. It was always about power. You know that."

He took a drag and looked out at where the black water from the Bronx flowed into the East River.

"Must be all of five years ago now. Russia was pushing its influence in Africa. You guys always thought of yourselves as the heirs to the British Empire, never mind the War of Independence. What's a little Oedipal in-fighting among empires? Keep it in the family. No problem. So as the British Empire faded, America stepped in to mop up Africa with a few trade concessions here and a few exclusive exploitation contracts there. And why not? We gave them hospitals, railways and fucking schools, why shouldn't we make something on the deal?"

He looked like he wanted an answer so I said, "Keep talking."

"But all these little upstart republics keep discovering fuckin' socialism and communism. And you know what? When all you've ever known is tribal kingdoms and the British Empire, socialism and communism make a lot more sense than bloody democracy. I mean, I'm President Cosmo Manuel of Cabinda-Itumba and you make me an offer, 'You can either have a multi-party system where the leader gets changed every four or five years, and the people get to vote and have guaranteed liberties, or you can have absolute power for life and the people shut up and do as they're told. Which do *you* think I'm going to go for?"

"So Russian-backed socialism was spreading in Africa. So what?"

"So the CIA sent a delegation to visit President Cosmo Manuel and told him, 'You guarantee our interests in Cabinda-Itumba, crush any filthy communist-backed movements, and we will make you a very rich, powerful man and put Cabinda-Itumba on the world stage."

"You know this or are you just speculating conspiracy theories?"

He gave me a small laugh and a pitying smile. "I was at the fucking meeting, mate. I saw the whole thing. I even recorded it. I've got the recordings at my apartment, on my fucking laptop."

He flicked ash using his ring finger and stared down between his feet.

"So the president promised the CIA men he would stamp out Russian-backed movements forever in Cabinda-Itumba. And he sent me and my boys of the Praetorian Guard to defend freedom and equality, and the sacred values of democracy, by annihilating the three main villages which were known to give succor to the communist rebels. We had experience doing that kind of thing. It wasn't the first village we'd exterminated over the years. So we got in the Land Rovers, we drove to the villages, tortured the townsfolk until they told us where the boys were, the rebels, and then we systematically killed everybody. It was pretty heavy, even for us. Couple of the lads were sick."

He looked at me suddenly, like he'd had a sudden thought. "You ever done extermination work?" I shook my head. "They tell you it gets easier. It doesn't. It gets harder every time you do it. And it stays with you." He poked at his head with his finger. "You dream about it, remember it in weird moments, like when you're in bed with your girl, and suddenly you remember their faces, and you can't perform. Fucks with your head."

"Your daughter's name is Adelina?"

He looked surprised at the question. "Yeah."

"Adelina dos Santos?"

"You're not going to use her to blackmail me, mate? You don't need to do that."

"We don't use blackmail, Jan. That's not how we do things. Is that her name?"

"Yeah, why?"

"For the file."

He didn't look convinced. "Right..."

"What was she doing there?"

A breeze blew in off the East River, bringing a slightly rancid smell of ozone. He considered me a moment, squinting his eyes. "What has that got to do with you, or anybody?"

"Next time you dodge a question I'm going to blow your kneecap off. Do I need to prove I mean it?"

He studied my face. "No."

"What was she doing at your apartment?"

"A few years ago, when she turned eighteen, I went to see her and told her who I was. I'd pulled strings all her life to make sure she went to the best schools, university, and got a good job—"

"Who does she work for? Why is she here in New York?"

"She works for Afro-American Petrochemicals. They have an office in New York and I got them to send her here. I figured it would be good for her, professionally, and open her up to the wider, Western world."

He flicked the cigarette butt out into the water, then scratched his head.

"It hadn't gone great when I told her I was her father. She'd accused me of a lot of shit. I tried to tell her I'd always kept an eye out for her and her mother, but she didn't buy it. Women, huh? All they want is absolutely everything." I didn't laugh and he went on. "Anyway, when she arrived in New York I asked her to come and see me, so we could talk and try and sort things out."

"Why are the CIA watching you?"

He didn't look surprised. "You won't be surprised to discover that the USA's promise to elevate Cabinda-Itumba to the international stage never materialized. It has always been, and still is, a small, poor country most people have never even heard of. So I took a trip recently to Moscow at the head of a trade delegation, and arranged a private meeting at the Kremlin. There, I suggested to several top officials that we could buy things in the Western marketplace which they could not, because of the international trade embargos against Russia. However, given the right inducements, we would be willing to do so and quietly sell them on to Moscow via the back door.

"The inducements in question were along the lines of Moscow providing us with the kind of weaponry and training that would, at last, make our presence felt in Africa, if not the wider world. I don't know if you are aware of this, but President Cosmo Manuel considers that there are areas along the coast which rightfully belong to his tribe. If he had them, that could make Cabinda-Itumba an international player.

"Obviously, the CIA were not pleased about our cozying up to the Russians, and they are mad at me. They hold me responsible and think I should be taught a lesson."

I was quiet for a long time, watching the sun turn copper on the small waves. Finally I asked him: "How many villages have you annihilated, Jan?"

He shrugged. I watched him pull another cigarette from the pack and poke it in his mouth. "Six, seven. I forget." He flicked his lighter and leaned into the flame. When the cigarette was alight I said, "The tide is rising." I jerked my head at where the water line had risen and was just a couple of feet from his boots. He stared at it a moment, and somehow he understood what it meant. He frowned at me and stood, spreading his hands. "Aw, come on, you said—"

"No, you said, Jan. All I said was we take care of things while providing credible deniability, and we pay the highest rates. This is your payment for annihilating…," I echoed his shrug, "six or seven villages."

I put the slug through his right frontal lobe, so it spun him slightly, turning his back to the water. So when he fell he fell toward the rising black tide. He lay there, with his feet higher than his head, staring wide-eyed at the sky, as the pulsing water gradually covered his face. Soon, during the dark hours of the night, as the tide receded, he would be dragged out to the deep.

On an impulse I moved down to where he was lying, took my handkerchief and stuffed it in his mouth. Then, using my Swiss Army knife I cut off a chunk of his hair, folded it in the handkerchief and put it in my pocket.

I reached in his jacket, found his cell and his keys and made my way back across the scrubland to where he'd parked. There I climbed behind the wheel and drove slowly up Soundview to the Bruckner Expressway, and retraced our steps to the parking garage under 166 East 35th Street. I left the car in his lot and his key in the glove compartment, and, after a moment's thought, made my way up to his apartment and let myself in.

I had a snoop around, but there was one thing in particular I was looking for and I found it in a small bedroom he'd adapted as a den. It was his laptop. Before taking it I searched the drawers in his desk for some kind of diary. I found it. It was long, slim, black and leather-bound, as you'd expect. I opened it and smiled. All his passwords were neatly laid out in alphabetical order. The more security the nerds force on us, the sloppier they force us to become.

Downstairs I retrieved my car and sat behind the wheel for a while growing steadily more mad. Finally I pulled my cell from my pocket and dialed. The brigadier answered.

"Yes, Harry."

"Job's done. Is the colonel with you?"

"No. Why?"

"I need to talk to her about this job."

"Was there a problem?"

"Yeah, you could say there was a problem."

"We'd better meet at my flat. Four twenty-eight, Riverside Drive." He gave me the number of the apartment and asked, "How serious is this, Harry? Is there some action I need to be taking?"

"I don't know until we talk to the colonel."

"All right, come on over. If you get here before she does you can tell me what it's about."

I went home to my brownstone on James Baldwin Place, showered and shaved and changed my clothes. I guess I wasn't that keen to tell the brigadier what it was all about before the colonel showed up. Finally, at about six in the evening I took my TVR and growled across Manhattan to Morningside Heights, and rode the antique elevator up to the top floor. The brigadier opened the door himself and arched an eyebrow at me.

"I expected you a little earlier."

"Yes, sir. But I thought the least I could do was change out of my work clothes and have a shave." I noted that he was wearing a sage green, paisley silk cravat. "Has the colonel arrived?"

"Some time ago. Whiskey?"

"Thank you."

I followed him into the drawing room. The brigadier was not the kind of man to have a living room, he had a drawing room, into which one withdrew to listen to music, read books and drink very expensive drinks. I had to pause. The entire west wall was taken up with two large windows and two sliding glass doors onto an ample terrace. On the terrace now, in a violet silk dress that did nothing to hide her legs, was the colonel, holding a tall gin and tonic. She was gazing out at Riverside Park, the vast, dark Hudson and the glimmering lights of Jersey across the water.

The colonel was pouring my drink and spoke over his shoulder. "I had a feeling this might happen, so I have booked a table at Keens."

"For you and the colonel?"

He went very still, then turned to face me. He handed me my drink.

"I am going to ignore that remark, Harry. It is unworthy of you. But don't do it again."

I took the drink and nodded once. "Yes sir."

He crossed the floor to the sliding doors and leaned out.

"Jane, would you like to join us?"

She turned, stepped inside and stared at me a moment. My belly was warm with adrenalin and I told myself it was because I was mad.

She said, "Hello, Harry."

I nodded and spoke quietly. "Colonel."

She lowered herself into a large, calico chair. "The brigadier said you wanted to talk to me."

The brigadier sat on the sofa. I remained standing.

"Yeah, I'd like to know if I am being used as a hit man for the CIA."

Her face might have been granite for all the expression it showed. She met my eye and held it. "Explain yourself!"

"I don't need to explain myself, Colonel. You gave me a job, I accepted it and I did it. You and your pals at the CIA had him under surveillance. So I think you need to explain to me why you told me he was alone, but when I got there he was with a woman. Did the Company think I was going to execute her for them too? Maybe you could explain to me also why I wasn't told the Company had him on a list to be punished for cozying up to the Russians. So no, I am not going to 'explain myself,' Colonel, but I think you should explain yourself. Are you using Cobra to execute contracts for the CIA?"

She sat very still and didn't say anything. I reached in my pocket and pulled out two plastic bags, which I dropped on the lamp table beside the brigadier. One contained Adelina's small plastic bottle. The other contained the handkerchief smothered in Jan's saliva and his hair.

"The woman left, having seen my face. You had better explain to the CIA that I do not kill innocent people just because they may be able to identify me. I let her go because I had to, as a matter of moral principle. So I took Jan in his own car to Sound-view Park, at the mouth of the Bronx River, and I made him talk. He told me a lot. Among other things he told me the girl was his daughter, her name is Adelina dos Santos and she works for Afro-American Petrochemicals." I pointed. "The handkerchief and the hair are his DNA. The bottle is her DNA. I want to know if she really is his daughter, I want a copy of the CIA file on him and I want to know if I have been played."

The room went quiet. The brigadier, usually quick to defuse any kind of tension, remained silent, looking down at the carpet, pursing his lips. The colonel's cheeks had turned a very attractive pink and I battled with myself to remain mad. After a moment she said, "Absolutely not."

I frowned at her. "Absolutely not, what? She is absolutely not his daughter, I absolutely cannot have a copy of the CIA file, or I absolutely cannot know if I have been played?"

She had added bright, moist eyes to her pink cheeks and was watching me with barely repressed fury. The brigadier said, "Why don't you sit down, Harry?"

He made it sound like the sanest thing to do in an insane world, so I did it. When I was safely seated and sipping my whiskey, he shifted his gaze to the colonel.

"Jane, you know you have my unconditional trust. That is how we operate. But you know also that it is not enough for justice to be done, it must be *seen* to be done. The fact is your operatives told you van Hoek was alone, when they must have known this woman was with him."

He didn't wait for her to answer. He reached for his phone, pressed a single number and after a moment said, "Send me a courier. I have some items for the lab." He hung up and made another call. "I am sending you two items. Label them A and B. A is the bottle. I want to know if the two people were related. Give it top priority. I want the results by morning."

He hung up again and looked at the colonel. There was resentment in her eyes when she returned his stare, and when she looked at me.

"I was not a part of the investigation into Jan van Hoek. I knew that the Company's interest in him centered around the rise of Russian influence in Africa, but nothing beyond that. A week ago the director had the file sent to me. He is the only person who knows about my secondment to Cobra. He called me and told me the CIA could not pursue the matter here in the States beyond simply observing the target, but that I should draw the man's record to the attention of the board at Cobra, to see if he was a suitable mark. And that is precisely what I did, Alex, with your approval, and the board unanimously agreed he should be executed."

The brigadier turned to me. "That is absolutely correct. I can vouch for every word."

I held the colonel's eye. "Why was I sent to hit van Hoek when there was a woman there with him? It could have cost me my life, and if you had sent a less experienced operative it could have cost an innocent woman *her* life. I don't believe they didn't know she was there. I don't believe the CIA are that sloppy."

"I don't know." She took a deep breath and added, "You are quite right. It should not have happened and I can assure you the CIA are *not* that sloppy. If it happened it was either a fluke or it was deliberate. Either way I'll find out and report back to you both."

I said, "Thank you. What about the copy of the file?"

She glanced at the brigadier. He frowned and cleared his throat. "What for, Harry? The job is done. There was an incident and we want to ensure it doesn't happen again. But snooping on CIA operations is not what we do, and it will set a very bad precedent."

I jerked my chin toward the two plastic bags on the lamp table beside him. "Why are you checking on van Hoek's DNA? Why do you want to know if she was his daughter?"

He gave his head a short, dismissive shake. "That is quite different, Harry. It has nothing to do with the CIA investigation. It is a legitimate part of our work to investigate the people closely related to a target, to see to what extent they are, or were, involved in the target's crimes."

I nodded and waited a moment, studying his face.

"Forgive me if I seem impertinent, sir, but I think you just answered your own question. I want to know to what extent the CIA were involved in van Hoek's crimes."

Scan the QR code below to purchase BLOOD ON BALTHAZAR.
Or go to: righthouse.com/blood-on-balthazar